The Mole Of Edge Hill:
The World of Williamson's Tunnels

David Clensy

© 2006 by David Clensy. All rights reserved.

Also by the author:

Island Life: A History Of Looe Island

Preface:

A Worthy Pioneer

"Well said, old mole! Canst work i' the earth so fast? A worthy pioneer!" **Hamlet, Act 1, scene v**

THERE was a book in our house when I was growing up that sparked my imagination. It was a flimsy little paperback filled with tales of the mysteries of Merseyside. There were all kinds of stories of ghosts and ghouls between the covers of that long lost book.

But the chapter that really caught my attention didn't seem to involve the supernatural at all.

It told the story, in the briefest terms, of Joseph Williamson, the so-called Mole Of Edge Hill. He was, it seemed, a rich Liverpool merchant, who two centuries ago paid a small army of men to secretively dig a labyrinth of tunnels beneath the expensive houses on the outskirts of the city.

The fact that the author of the little paperback had only devoted a couple of pages to Williamson's remarkable story had the effect of leaving my puzzled young mind with more questions than answers.

Why did Williamson want these tunnels? Was it really the first job creation scheme, as many people thought? Was he some kind of bizarre troglodyte, living out his subterranean fantasies? Was he compelled by charity, by religion, or by some sort of mysterious cult?

The thought even crossed my mind that he may have been constructing some kind of top secret government arsenal. This was, after all, an era when enemies seemed to lurk at every turn – both outside and within the country.

The British had recently witnessed, and indeed fought through, the Napoleonic wars, while the lessons of the French Revolution were being taken extremely seriously by the authorities in this country.

But surely such a scheme couldn't have left posterity with no official records of its existence?

Maybe Williamson just liked tunnels.

Whatever the reason, Williamson and his tunnels remained at the back of my mind throughout my childhood.

But it was as a student of cultural history at Liverpool John Moore's University, some years later, that I really began to learn more about this mysterious man, focusing as I did, my final year degree dissertation on Williamson's tunnels.

After graduating I left my home city to study for an MA at Cardiff, and in the years that followed my career as a journalist took me far and wide.

But still my thoughts returned to the Mole Of Edge Hill.

It always struck me as being rather peculiar that this singular figure of Liverpool's past should not be immortalised in any great detail with a book about his life.

Well fear not dear reader, for now he has. Indeed, you are holding that very book in your hands.

For the past seven years an unhealthy amount of my free time has been spent in the company of a mysterious tobacco merchant who left this world almost two centuries ago, leaving behind him a peculiar warren of tunnels.

And in fact I have penned not one, but two books in his honour. Both of the works are to be found within these pages.

Which is where I start to run an admittedly dangerous line between fact and fiction.

The first half of this book is a short novella in which I imagine what Williamson's existence might have been like.

The second half of the book is a true history of the man and his tunnels – perhaps the most in-depth examination of the Mole Of Edge Hill yet penned.

But please, don't confuse the two. While most of the novella is based on the things we know about Williamson's life, I have also weaved in elements of my own creation, and stories from other snippets of Lancashire folklore.

I make no apology about this. For the greatest legacy of Williamson is not in fact his tunnels, but his myth, and the folklore that has developed around him.

The beauty of myth and folklore is that it grows with each generation, and I'm happy to play a part in that living process.

Rest assured however that there is no such playing with the facts in the second half of the book, when the true story of Williamson's Tunnels will be fully revealed.

More often than not, it's far more bizarre than the fiction.

David Clensy, June 2006

The Mole Of Edge Hill

1840

THE tortured steam rushed from the engine in a blast. The great metal wheels creaked into life.

Slowly at first, the train muscled its way out of the station. An elderly man wandered along the platform, a whistle to his lips. Somewhere a clock struck.

Steam and smog merged into one great thick soup as the train made its way through the labyrinth of chimneys and terraces.

From below, among the cholera and cobbles, a shabbily dressed child peered up from a soot-blackened face, and revealed her smile.

Another scream, and Manchester retreated with all due reverence through the smudge stained windows of the carriage.

A tall, thin young man lifted off a hat, which was a little out of fashion, and placed it on the cushioned seat. He settled a bundle of papers carefully beside it and sat down.

A middle-aged woman sat opposite him, and a vicar seated beside her dozed into an elaborately folded newspaper.

"It's wonderful is it not?" the woman offered, almost as if to nobody, and the young man replied with an acknowledging smile.

"I was lucky enough to be on the first run that was made."

"Really?" he said.

There was a prolonged pause, before she went on: "Are you from the old town yourself Mr...."

"Trelawny."

"...Mr Trelawny?"

"No, in fact I live just over there," he said pointing vaguely to half of the city.

"But Trelawny surely is a Cornish name?"

"Yes. My family originally comes from the West Country, but I've only known Manchester. I write for the Manchester Guardian."

"Really?" she enthused. "How wonderful. My name's Kemble. I could tell you some remarkable tales for your newspaper."

"I am sure you could Mrs Kemble. We do see some things in this city."

"Yes indeed," she agreed thoughtfully, before beginning again. "Huskisson. Does that name mean anything to you? No, too young no doubt. But he was killed poor man, on that very first journey that we made when they opened the line from Liverpool."

"That's right, I do recall the incident now," Richard said. "He was a politician?"

"Yes. Lady Wilton said that she distinctly heard the crushing of the bone. You can put that in your Manchester Guardian no doubt sir."

"I fear we may be a little too late – it must be at least ten years ago."

"Yes, almost exactly in fact. I was just thinking of it when I climbed aboard. The date is ingrained on my memory I am afraid – the 15th of September 1830, if I am not much mistaken, and I very rarely am Mr…"

"Trelawny."

"…Trelwany, yes. Very rarely. But of course then I was a young girl. Terribly excited too. My mother considerably dampened the *occasion by being frightened to death. Not to mention the unfortunate end that Mr Huskisson met of course."*

"Of course."

"Yes, well that completely ruined the day. Still it was something to see the Duke of Wellington in a stir."

"I'm sure Napoleon would have thought much the same madam."

"Indeed. Indeed."

The scene outside had transformed itself into a pastoral landscape, and field after field flew past as the conversation droned on.

It was still droning on as the train reached the outskirts of Liverpool. Row-upon-row of red brick terrace slums passed the window once again.

The locomotive hissed loudly as it turned a corner, and entered the sudden darkness of a tunnel cut straight into a rock face.

Mrs Kemble continued talking, but Richard Trelawny was barely listening. The vicar was still sleeping.

"Well, while I was chewing the cud of this disappointment, which was rather bitter, I can tell you Mr…"

"Trelawny."

"Yes, well, I had imagined her to be as delighted as myself with our excursion you see. Anyway, it was at that moment that a man flew by us calling out through a speaking-trumpet to stop the engine…"

Richard managed to appear vaguely interested while also peering out of the window at the intricate brickwork of the tunnel, barely visible in the dim light.

Each stone was covered in a green mildew, and tiny plants were crowding in the cracks.

Poor doomed creatures, he thought. How odd it is where things will grow.

He observed how they were stretching wistfully to the side to face the light from the tunnel entrance in their vertical bed.

Things will always fight to survive, he told himself. Even the most wretched of these isolated plants is alive, even here in this gloom. Cold and alone deep beneath the surface of the earth.

But he smiled to see that even in these conditions one of the weeds proudly displayed a single brilliant yellow flower.

The undaunted pride of the flower that is never seen, he muttered. Would it stand so proud, he wondered, if it knew of the world above the rocks, where other flowers sway in meadows, and ornament the sweeping hillside, a gentle breeze flowing through their petals. The sun warm on their tender stamen. The light bright on their supple stem – he was amusing himself with mock heroic language.

Yet here in this constant night it thinks it is in heaven, he added to himself. A proud narcissus charmed by his own image reflected from the train windows.

"And yet I am probably the first to have seen him," *he said aloud, to the vague bewilderment of Mrs Kemble.*

"Well, quite." *she agreed.* "Oh, but you should have heard Mrs Huskisson's piercing shriek, yet not a sound was heard, nor a word uttered among the spectators of the catastrophe. Oh, and what a catastrophe. I don't know much about politics, but I do know…"

Richard thought gently to himself in spite of Mrs Kemble as finely cut brick after brick passed by the window.

But for a moment the pattern changed. Briefly, high up in the side of the tunnel the brickwork was different, less regular. A circle stood out in the steep face of the tunnel – a patch devoid of plant life.

It was difficult to say, but it seemed that Mrs Kemble's conversation continued a little after Richard had stood up and stepped off the train, walked out of the station, and on into the hectic street outside.

Liverpool was alive. It was slimy cobbles, and galloping horses. Cheeky boys in oversized rags thick with the dirt of a world unwashed. It was coughing cracked gas lamps, and wheezing old men. Elegant buildings huddling together snugly in a peaceful embrace, as carriages creaked, and seagulls shrieked a malignant refrain, and the rain touched the soul with an icy sting.

Liverpool fell steeply, bowed towards the gunmetal peaks of the Mersey waves, which lapped, in a constant fury between a hundred vessels of every possible form.

Their sails billowed across the skyline for the full extent of Richard's vision. Great bows lurched menacingly towards the docksides. Miles of thick stubborn rope peopled the quays in twists and swirls, and smelled like the thickest coffee brewing on the warmest of days.

Richard moved steadily down through the narrow streets skipping sideways to avoid a stray dog that snarled from some backstreet darkness.

The world was an eclectic mix of slum and splendour. Wealth and poverty rubbed shoulders as they went about their lives.

Great columned and façaded buildings towered over creaky wooden shacks where men with whiskers like blankets sold fruit.

Beside a hectic red-bricked warehouse Richard tripped through the inky puddles of an alleyway that opened out onto a square of unworshiped buildings.

On the far side of Wolstenholme Square there stood a tobacco company building. Richard walked inside and approached a bespectacled old man who seemed to have his head buried in the middle of his chest.

"I'm looking for Mr Moss-Tate."

"Are you?" *he replied with vague interest.*

"Is he around at all?"

"Yes. Yes he will be I would have thought. Do you have an appointment sir?"

"No."

"Oh. Well it doesn't really matter anyway. He's in that office over there."

Richard neglected to thank the man. He walked across the empty room and knocked on the door. There was no response. He knocked again. And this time there was a sort of bark from behind the oak, so Richard opened it and ventured inside.

"Mr Moss-Tate?"

An elderly man looked over thin-rimmed spectacles and grunted.

Richard went on: "I'm looking for a Mr Williamson actually sir – I thought that you might be able to help."

"Well you certainly won't find him here," *the old man snorted.* "You'll be lucky to find him anywhere."

"But Mr Williamson did work here once?"

"He did, once. And then he stopped working here the day he started owning the place."

"Do you know Mr Williamson personally?"

"I'd say I knew him as well as any man could but do not presume sir that is saying much. He's my brother-in-law, and a fine, noble, difficult, strange little man he is. And why, may I ask do you want to see him?"

"I have come to talk to him about the tunnels," Richard said with a stammer. "We have heard great things in Manchester about the man's peculiar fascination for building tunnels. I am interested in seeing them."

The old man laughed into his chest. "Philanthropy, not madness," he announced grandly. "Mark my words sir. Philanthropy, not madness."

By the time he'd finished coughing out the sentence a number of times the old man had written a few lines of scrolling words onto a scrap of paper.

There was a brief discussion about the weather, before the old man laughed a little louder than was reasonable. Unnerved by this cackle Richard left the tobacco merchants with the scribbled address. It was raining heavily.

***

1818

The sun was bright against the newly whitewashed walls of the barn on Mason Street.

A carpenter sat straddled across the eaves gently tapping away, causing a shower of chippings to float down on the breeze, and out across the cobbled street. The amber flecks of twisted shavings fell like confetti upon the freshly laid cobbles, and were trampled under foot by a horse, which galloped along the street pulling a great black two seater buggy in its wake.

The horse stopped abruptly outside a formidable newly painted home near to the end of the street, and a heavy-set barrel-chested figure stormed out of the buggy and up the steps.

The man marched through the doorway and disappeared inside. He was followed by a sedate lady in a violet dress and purple cloak.

She revealed an elegant face which would once have been pretty but had grown sternly attractive with middle age. She smiled at a man who was walking along the street carrying a large parcel. He smiled back, and touched his cap as he walked by.

Inside a parlour maid cringed her shoulders with fear as she took the man's coat and hat, and quickly tottered away down the hallway.

"Don't worry Mabel, he's in one of his tempers." The lady explained as she followed him in.

"I'm well used to his tempers Mrs Williamson," An elderly woman chuckled as she removed the lady's cloak and folded it across her arm. "It's young Mary who quivers in her shoes."

The lady laughed a little, followed her husband into the parlour, and closed the door.

"Now you calm down Joseph," she said sternly. "You're frightening the servants."

"Calm down!" Williamson gasped, "I'll give you bloody calm down young missy." He seethed, "I'll calm you down by God, I'll have you calmed down in your grave the way you're heading."

Williamson's face was crimson. His crumpled complexion twisted in his rage, and his balding scalp sparkled as the sun shone upon it through the window.

"I'll give you bloody calm! The next time you humiliate me in such a way, by God I'll horse-whip you all the way back to your father's house and leave you for dead."

"I merely gave my opinion."

"You've no bloody right to give your opinions woman. You made a fool of me, and no mistake. I spent the best part of the last twenty years working to make good my dealings with other merchants and know what can and can not be said in such circumstances."

"But I was merely repeating what you had said yourself."

"Said myself, aye, said myself in the privacy of my own bloody home to my own bloody wife, never expecting her to go out and start preaching a load of abolitionist clap trap in the company of gentlemen."

"Joseph I only said…"

"I know what you said woman - I was there."

"It's more than ten years since they abolished it."

"Ten years aye. Ten years as maybe. But ten years for those men of falling profit. Ten years of fewer ships and falling wages. Ten years of war and misery. By God you've no right to spout politics,"

"But…"

"Even if I've been the one to tell you it."

The young maid entered the room with a tray. The teapots and plates rattled as she walked. The lady smiled at her and a caged bird tweeted in the otherwise silent room.

"Don't worry Mary, you'll get used to Mr Williamson's rages."

Mary placed the tray down, gave a nervous curtsy and left the room closing the door behind herself.

Williamson roared into the chimney breast, and slobbered across his chin as he raged.

Elizabeth sat pertly in a chair and listened courteously to her husband's rantings. She was quite used to them, and knew very well how to sit them out.

Williamson lifted up the tray and threw it into the fireplace. The teapot exploded in a shower of porcelain, and the cups, saucers and plates landed in a broken mess.

Elizabeth slowly raised an eyebrow and continued to smile politely.

"Smile at me will you?" he roared, and bounded over to the birdcage. He picked the brass cage up and strode purposefully out of the back door, and down into the garden.

He opened the latch on the cage and placed it on the floor. He then strode across to an aviary which stood on the other side of the lawn and flung open the doors. One by one the colourful, timid little birds escaped and flew around the lawn.

The canary eventually followed suit and left its brass cage.

The garden looked Eden-like, with the tropical menagerie flying around, as Williamson stood in the centre of the lawn and raged, his face burning like fire.

He cried up into the air bitterly: "There! See how the poor devils like to get free. Many a married man would like to have wings and the doors of wedlock thrown open so that they might fly away and be at rest."

He then strode off away from the house, and disappeared through a gate.

Elizabeth calmly walked across to the fireplace and started to pick up the smashed porcelain.

***

Williamson tramped down the alleyway like a spoilt child. As he walked across the cobbles he snorted and coughed.

At the Fox and Hounds he sat alone in a dimly-lit corner with a flagon of porter and the face of a grimly descending temper.

One young man raised a cap to him as he walked through the front door, but Williamson simply huffed and shuffled a little closer to the fireplace.

A pair of old yellow eyes watched him carefully from the shadows.

After a second drink he stood up and wandered out of the door, blankly ignoring the goodnights of the landlord.

With splutters and snorts and groans he walked back up the rain-washed hill and shuffled into the house like a shamed schoolboy.

Noticing his wife stood at the bottom of the staircase, his shuffle reignited into a stomp. He pushed past her muttering, "By God aye, we'll have no more of this."

He walked theatrically up the stairs, leaving Elizabeth smiling in recognition of how well she knew her husband.

***

The following morning saw a quiet breakfast table. Elizabeth at one end and Williamson at the other.

Jam was spread across toast in silence. Tea was poured in silence. Eggs were eaten in silence.

The silence was only broken by the steady ticking of the clock, and the delicate twittering of the canary, who was happy to be back behind the brass bars of his cage – as was Williamson, although he cared not to show it. It was necessary to show Elizabeth that his anger was still burning.

However as the breakfast came to an end he walked out of the room, and paused to place his hand on her shoulder momentarily in a silent act of conciliation.

Elizabeth smiled. She knew that all would be back to normal by that evening.

Williamson took his cane from Mary, who was stood in a practised manner in the hall. She helped him on with an overcoat and handed him a top hat.

He strode out of the house with a manly gait.

As he walked purposefully along Mason Street Williamson noticed two ladies edging towards him in whispers. One looked like the sort of middle aged spinster that Williamson held a particular disdain for, but she accompanied a younger lady with a bright and pretty face that returned his gaze with an equality of confidence.

As they approached Williamson piped-up, "Whispers for women, merriment for men, that will bring Satan straight out of his den."

The ladies looked at him with fear and curiosity respectively.

He continued: "A whispering crow, and a cackling hen, will mean that the devil will something, something again."

Williamson had lost face, and it showed graphically upon his own.

"I'm not sure that was right," the fresh faced confident lady said with a mocking sterness.

"Well, perhaps not." Williamson conceded, "But you know what I mean."

"No," she replied, "Frankly I don't. But you may be of more use than you look – I'm looking for a gentleman of these parts called Williamson."

"Really?" Williamson said scratching his face with a puzzled expression.

"Have you heard of Mr Williamson?"

"Well, yes I think I may know the man, madam. Why would you be looking for him."

"To damn your impertinence I think," she snapped. "I have been told that he owns a lot of the property at Edge Hill."

"Well, yes, I think you could be right there – a fine man I've heard, young and handsome and remarkably rich."

"So it is true – he would be the man to see about moving into a house at Edge Hill?"

"Well I would think so madam, but what is the attraction in Edge Hill for a young and fashionable lady such as yourself?"

"You really are beyond belief sir. But if you must ask such questions, I was advised by my physician that the air up here on the hill is finer than any in the whole of Lancashire. But since meeting you I have become uncertain."

Williamson failed to withhold a momentary snigger, "Williamson is certainly the man you are looking for – his land runs from Miss Mason's property in the north, to Grinfield Street in the south, and from Mason Street at its eastern-most border to Smithdown Lane in the West."

"Really?"

"Yes. His houses are the finest in the land, I'll warrant. I know madam because I am a humble worker of the great man."

"Right – well you can show me some rooms, I needn't bother Mr Williamson personally."

Moments later the curious-looking trio were stood in a ranging old house at the top of Mason Street.

"Oh no, this will never do at all," the lady announced. "Never at all."

At that point the door opened and a group of Irish navvies wandered in with a bundle of timber on their backs. Seeing the group in the middle of the room, they stopped and removed their caps.

"Oh, excuse us Mr Williamson, sir – we were just fixing these stairs, sir."

The younger woman let out an angry yelp, like a dog having its paws trodden on. For a moment she stood with hands on hips, glaring at Williamson.

Her companion started to hide herself even closer behind her back, and then followed her as she stormed out without saying another word.

Williamson chased after them, giving the carpenter a tardy slap around the head as he went.

He scampered along Mason Street. By the time he reached her he was laughing. She stopped and gave another angry yelp.

"I really am very sorry madam – I'm afraid I couldn't resist it."

"Well you are no gentleman sir – you are a bounder and a cad and…"

"Will you please accept my humblest apology," Williamson offered bending down onto one knee with a theatrical flurry.

The lady's eyes relaxed a little, and she let out another hiss, before nodding a little and admitting, "Well, yes, I will forgive you this time Williamson – but only because I'm so keen to live at Edge Hill. On a personal level I think you are little more than an idiot."

"Thank you madam, I am forever indebted, Mrs?"

"Henderson." She said with renewed firmness, "Miss Henderson."

"Tell me Miss Henderson, what accommodation did you have in mind?"

"Well certainly not this barren and ugly thing," she said, looking up at the house with a mixture of disgust and a retained angry embarrassment.

"What then Miss Henderson, would suit you?"

"Why, one with three parlours, six bedrooms, and every convenience."

"Really, madam? And how much would you be willing to pay for such a fine home?"

A serious look swept across her face, and she looked to the ground like a child, "I could pay thirty pounds a year sir,"

Williamson erupted into riotous laughter. He wheezed from the very pit of his belly, and tears welled in his eyes.

Between delighted gasps for oxygen he mockingly bellowed, "One with three parlours, six bedrooms, and every convenience – for thirty pounds a year!"

Emily Henderson's face was crimson, and she felt a welling anger deep within her chest. She clenched her fists together, looked to the floor with a frowning brow and pouted extravagantly.

Williamson, who was continuing to amuse himself, called over a group of his workers and sarcastically announced, "This fine and generous lady is prepared to pay me thirty pounds a year for a house with three parlours, six bedrooms, and…" he gave a sweeping 'wait for it' arm gesture before adding, "…every convenience."

The workers laughed loudly in a show of loyalty, until all noticed a tear welling in Emily Henderson's soft blue eyes. There was a dying murmur as it crept gently out of her eye and wandered woefully down her delicate red cheek.

Defeated, she turned and ran down the street. Her companion picked one of the workers at random and slapped him sharply across the face, before running after her.

Williamson dropped his cane and ran in pursuit. Before very long Williamson tired and slowed to a walk, but he discovered Emily

Henderson sat on the edge of a cart, being comforted by the hen-like woman.

"I'll see you on Thursday Miss Henderson," He said, "I think you will come." Williamson turned and walked back up Mason Street.

A moment later Emily Henderson coughed out in angry tearful gasps, "Never in a million years you dog!"

***

Richard slipped across the cobbled streets, pulling his hat down on to his head, and wrapping his jacket about himself as he went.

A boy sat, sheltering inside a doorway from the rain. He was wearing a sort of rag, draped across his shoulders and over his knees. He shivered a little, and coughed out visible condensation in short staccato yelps. It gave him the appearance of a long beleaguered dragon waiting for death in a half-imagined cave.

Richard wondered what time it was as he made his way quickly through a mud-soaked alleyway.

He came out in a place where men in thick overcoats smoked pipes. They huddled themselves into their own carriage, a whip held out towards the horse without any real conviction.

Richard climbed up onto one of the cabs. He handed the driver the wet paper. The driver had some difficulty deciphering the letters from the ink blotches that had streaked down in a swirling motion.

Eventually he seemed to realise what it said, cleared his throat loudly, then cracked the whip across the horse's saturated ears, and the carriage rumbled into life. It creaked around a cobbled bend and disappeared between two high-sided buildings.

The other drivers puffed on their pipes, paying little attention.

A few minutes later the carriage was heading up a steep hill. The rain had worsened and was moving sideways in great forks of water, heading straight into the horse's face.

It turned its nose to one side, a horrified expression in its frowning eyes, and moved steadily up the hill.

Richard shivered a little. His wet clothes seemed to send icy stabs into his body, and the carriage rocked and shook as it moved over cobbled street after cobbled street.

Eventually the cab ground to a halt and the horse snorted with disgust. Richard stepped outside into the rain, and looked around.

"This is the road sir," the driver told him. Richard smiled, and reached into his pockets for some change. He paid the driver, over tipped him, and picked up his battered old leather case.

He stepped off the cobbles and headed up Mason Street.

Edge Hill was only a small suburb of the city, distant and removed out in the Lancashire countryside, but it still had a metropolitan atmosphere.

Mason Street was an impressive line of sturdy homes. Large, sprawling buildings each with an imposing separate door just for coaches to be driven through, to keep them out of the weather.

Each house had a fine frontage, and elegant steps leading up to a brass encrusted heavy door.

And each had a long and elaborate garden at the rear. Richard caught the occasional glimpse of these through cracks in the carriage doorways.

Eventually he reached number 44. So this was it, Richard thought, looking up at the building. It stood tall and impressive in the gas-lit evening. This was the home of Williamson.

Richard gathered his thoughts for a moment, before walking calmly up the steps, and lifting the door knocker.

He knocked twice, and waited. Nobody came. He knocked again. Still no response.

Richard stepped back away from the door, and noticed a grid on the ground. He knelt for a closer look. But all he could see was darkness.

He stood up and brushed himself down. As he walked further along the street, a boy scurried past. Richard stopped the child and asked after Williamson. The boy pointed down the street.

A few minutes later Richard arrived at Smithdown Lane. Following the boy's directions he reached a dark passageway, leading away from the road.

At the end of the passage there was a vault of fine brickwork arching over the entrance to a great black tunnel. It funnelled down into darkness.

Richard looked into the tunnel, and could make out three archways. He ventured inside but it was too dark to carry on.

***

Thursday came, and Emily Henderson found herself stood on the edge of Mason Street, angry at herself for coming.

Williamson walked up to her and removed his hat.

"I think I owe you an apology madam."

"Yes."

"Indeed, for I was wrong, it seems that we may have a property to suit you." With this Williamson led her to the same house that she had been humiliated in front of the week before.

She frowned a deep and meaningful frown. But Williamson managed to encourage her to enter the building. Some of her spirit had gone, and she was still secretly keen to live on the hill.

Upon walking inside Williamson revealed three parlours one by one, which had been built by erecting three new walls to subdivide the original room.

He then took her upstairs to reveal six new bedrooms that had appeared in the space where there had formerly been three large rooms.

The whole house was elaborately furnished with drapes and furniture, rugs and wallpapers. A grandfather clock ticked calmly in the hall.

Emily was wide-eyed, and speechless with wonder.

Williamson placed a set of house keys into her hand. He whispered, "And all for thirty pounds a year," and walked out of the front door.

***

It was night, and the Williamson house was shrouded in silence, broken only by the steady ticking of the grandfather clock.

Throughout the house, maid and mistress alike writhed gently in sleep, lost in dreams.

Williamson lay staring at the ceiling. From within the knotted wooden beams, he believed for a moment that he saw a face.

It smiled down upon him in a sort of knowing way. He saw the mouth, and the worn, unkempt ragged beard and the once angry, now resigned eyes of a man lost to his cause.

The Rock stood before him now like a man, and beckoned slowly. Williamson followed.

Saint Peter's hands were rugged and brown. Not the hands of a tax collector at all, but in the dewy brown eyes of the Galilean, Williamson could see the reflection of Our Lord upon the cross, in the agony of crucifixion.

The wound across his ribcage wept, where the spear had swiped the life away from his heart, and his crippled arms shook violently at the shoulders. His feet were torn through with rusted nails, and there was terror in the eyes of the ebbing prophet.

The vomiting had stopped. The bleeding had waned. And now the sky erupted with rain, and to the lightening-strewn night he raised his thorny head in a final twisted flail and asked in a long forgotten tongue, "Father, why hast thou forsaken me?"

His beard then fell upon his chest, and the bloodied cry of hopelessness, ebbed into the wretched night, upon the barren hillside.

From a view across the ancient streets of Jerusalem, and surrounded by the lifeless hanging bodies of thieves, he closed his eyes upon the world for the final time.

Distant in the night sky, high above, Williamson followed a light across Gethsemane, where he saw from the edge of a void the brightly lit clock face reflecting upon the granite waves.

Watching over time itself he saw the winged figures of Griffin-like creatures, talons clinging delicately to hope.

He saw buildings of the future and of the past, and upon the Mersey the bloodied scent of human cargo.

Shielding his eyes from the cries of young boys in chains, he watched in horror the line of men trudge across the battle-torn plains of France.

Walking home in weariness and finding Liverpool a fate worse than death – where depression ebbed across the Earth, and homeless, penniless, jobless mirth thrived in the disease filled streets.

Where children died hungry and naked and without a cross, but with only agony and suffering and hopelessness.

And there beneath the shadowy cloak of night upon the cobbles of Wolstenhome Square, an urchin coughed out his final breaths – which showed themselves guiltily on ethereal wisps.

The vomiting had stopped. The bleeding had waned. And now the sky erupted with rain, and to the thunder lighted night he raised his tiny head in a final twisted flail and asked in a guttural dockside accent, "Father, why hast thou forsaken me?"

From a view across the port's ancient streets, and surrounded by the lifeless slumped bodies of thieves, he closed his eyes upon the world for the final time.

And in the knotted wooden beams, among his swirling wretched dreams, Williamson saw Saint Peter cry, across the inky charcoal sky.

***

Richard placed the leather case on the ground, and rummaged inside it, before lifting out a rickety gas lamp.

Back inside the vaulted passage he took a box of matches from his jacket pocket, and lit the lamp.

Holding it before him, he ventured into the darkness. The first archway led to nothing. A blank rock face met him just a few yards in. He came back out into the vaulted passage, and tried the second. It sloped steadily for a hundred yards, before opening into a small chamber.

Richard looked around, tilting the lamp against the walls to view the intricate brickwork. Delicate arches criss-crossed above his head.

As he stepped to the side Richard kicked against a piece of metal – the top rung of a ladder, leading down into a hole.

He looked down, but could see nothing. A glance back over his shoulder showed no light from the passage – the steepness of the passage meant the entrance was now obscured.

Richard took a deep breath, and holding the torch above his head, he slowly climbed down the ladder.

It descended further than Richard had imagined, but eventually he reached the bottom.

He could see three vaulted passages heading in different directions. Two seemed to be inclined downwards, while the other stretched upwards, and was less elaborately constructed. It had walls cut straight from the rock, and had only been adorned with brick archways at intervals.

Richard became nervous. He looked into one of the downward tunnels, and wondered what might be beyond the corner. Taking a deep, excited breath, he started down the passage.

He scampered along the tawny earth. Each turn brought a new image of unreal dimness, and each tunnel ended with a decision as it branched out in finger-like passages, groping ever deeper.

As Richard reached the end of another brickworked passage he saw only darkness ahead of him. He stopped a moment, looked back over his shoulder, and continued down into the damp-tasting, muddy air.

At the end of the passage there was a flight of steps cut into the bare rock. As he walked out onto the first step his breath left his body in a moment of intense vertigo. A vast gloomy chasm was open before him like a breach in the crust of the planet.

Richard's footsteps echoed through the chamber and reverberated back along the passageways, as he walked down the steps.

At the bottom of the steps he stood still for a moment, and stared around the room in fascination. The cavern was decorated like a great subterranean banqueting hall.

A table stood grandly before him. The silver candlesticks reflected the light from his torch, and twinkled at him as water dripped down onto them from the ceiling high above.

Richard looked at the ceiling as if examining the Sistine Chapel. For sixty or seventy feet above his head the roof of the chasm was decorated with long, ornate stalactites. They reached down like crystal chandeliers.

The great icicle-like pendants of calcium carbonate also twinkled down at the flame as if a reflection of the candlesticks below.

Richard stumbled through the cavern, past the great oak table and chairs, past an ornate gilded clock, a sturdy drinks cabinet, and a tray of crystal glasses.

He wandered past luxurious leather settees and chaise lounge, damp and sodden with water dripping through the rocks overhead.

The walls were hung with great tapestries, and an occasional stuffed animal could be seen emerging from the solid rock.

Richard felt a sudden chill, and moved towards a ramp at the edge of the room. He made his way out through an archway high in the side of the rock face wall, and chose not to look back.

At the end of another long vaulted passage he reached a spiral staircase cut into the rock. He began walking up the steps, feeling a powerful breeze from above.

The torch flickered, and died. All was darkness again.

***

"It is finished sir," the wild-eyed foreman said as he wiped a thin veneer of porter from his beard and slammed the tankard onto Williamson's desk.

Williamson frowned. "Finished?" he growled, "I don't think so Brown – go and get it done."

Brown looked to the floor in confusion. "But it is all done sir. Miss Henderson's staircase has been finished for days. The wall at the edge of Miss Mason's property has not only been replaced – it is twice the wall it was. And all the houses on the south side of the street have been finished for months sir."

"What about the arbours?"

"All done sir."

"The whatnots?"

"The whatnots surpass anything I have seen decorate a corner in my life sir. But they are all done. Should I finish the men up?"

"What about the fountains?"

"Fountains sir?"

"Jesus, Mary and all the blessed saints!" Williamson raged, "Don't tell me you've forgotten the fountains!"

"Fountains, sir?"

"Fountains? Fountains? Did I not specifically order you to build an ornate stone fountain in each and every garden?"

"Well, not as far as I can recall sir?"

"Not as far as you can recall. Not as far as that eh? Do you think I am a cheap man Brown?"

"Why, no sir."

"No sir. Do you think any house of my building would be without a fountain, Brown?"

"Why, no of course not sir."

"No of course not sir," Williamson said mockingly, "Well what are you doing drinking porter in my study when there is important work to be done."

"Erm."

"Erm nothing Brown. Do your men not like their wage?"

"Yes sir."

"Did it not save them and theirs from sure starvation after the war Brown?"

"Yes sir. Yes of course it did."

"Then be gone. I want fountains."

Brown left the room, tripping over his feet as he went.

"Great things will rise forth from those gardens Brown!" Williamson shouted after the foreman. But he was gone.

***

The weeks passed, and Williamson's masons produced some of the most splendid fountains that the people of Edge Hill had ever seen.

On a bright September afternoon, Elizabeth was sipping tea as Williamson stomped across the room, with an apparent urge to remind himself of the sound of the floorboards.

He hesitated on one, which made a slight creaking noise, looked down at it, and shook his head disappointedly.

"Joseph, I spoke to Miss Henderson this morning."

"Mmm." Williamson groaned, his mind still clearly on the floorboards.

"She asked me if you had ever spent time in the desert as a young man."

"What?"

"She told me, that if she ever sees another fountain she is likely to drown herself in it."

"Damnation." Williamson blurted obscurely.

There was a silence between the couple. The clock ticked gently.

"Joseph, she now has seven fountains in her garden alone."

"Humph."

"What is this obsession with fountains Joseph?" She asked, keeping the same, emotionless chirp in her voice.

Williamson responded with a piercing shriek of "Damnation!" before storming from the room.

Marching down the road in his rage he came upon a group of his men putting the finishing touches to a twelve-foot high fountain with ornate carvings of elk around its edge.

Williamson pushed the workers away from the work of art. He picked up a sledgehammer and thrust it into one of the elk.

The bulbous head of the stone beast shattered down the ridge of the nose, and with a second thud crumbled to the floor.

The men looked aghast at Williamson. Then looked at each other nervously.

Williamson handed the sledgehammer to Brown.

"Now I want you to destroy the lot," he boomed.

"But sir, they have cost you a fortune sir."

"The lot," he cried as he trudged away.

***

"Why do you do it, Joseph?" Elizabeth asked over breakfast.

"Hell woman what are you whimpering about now?"

"What was the point of the fountains Joseph?"

"They are life-giving fountains you stupid woman," he snuffled. But Elizabeth remained obviously confused, "Look Elizabeth. If you give them something to do, no matter what, it keeps them out of mischief."

"Mischief?"

"Aye, mischief and more besides I'd warrant."

Elizabeth sipped her tea. She knew better than to argue.

"And what's more," he added, "They are fifty men with families of four or five tykes each, at least. And a wife if she's not dead already." Suddenly candid, Williamson added, "If I let them go, what would become of them?"

Elizabeth looked upon her husband as never before. Lit gently by the morning sun, washing through the window, he looked for a moment like a tired, long-serving horse. Nostrils flared. Eyes big and brown and dewy.

"Damnation!" he roared, returning back to the Williamson that Elizabeth knew and loved, "I'll sack the lot then!"

Elizabeth sipped her tea.

***

He didn't sack a single one. He went straight out and gave each man a tankard of porter, before speaking to them like a great old battlefield general.

"Men, I have a most important task for you today. Most important. It must be conducted with great care and attention.

"If I find any man to be not working to his full potential he will be out on his ear. Understand? Out on his ear."

He pointed to a great lawn at the rear of Miss Mason's property, below them as they stood on the edge of the road.

"Dig it up," He said, "I want to see a hole there of twenty-five feet in depth. I want it shored up as safely as if it were a passage to damnation itself do you hear?"

The men nodded sombrely, and soon were digging with enthusiasm on the lawn.

***

A week later Miss Mason's lawn had become an abyss, shored up with intricately joined beams and planks.

Williamson handed Brown a tankard of porter and poured one for himself.

"I was not always thus you know Brown." He said with a hint of misery in his voice. "No. Joseph Williamson was born a poor tyke. A poor tyke indeed he was." He explained as if talking about a different man.

"Born into poverty on the tenth day of March, in the year 1769, in the town of Warrington. Have you ever seen Warrington Brown?"

Brown shook his head.

"Well you've not missed much there. I left it at the tender age of eleven you know Brown? Sent me packing to the old town. To Liverpool. To earn a living for myself, and by God I did that didn't I, my man?"

"Yes sir. You've certainly done that sir."

"I obtained a junior position in a tobacco company on Wolstenholme Square, owned by old Mr Tate.

"I came to Liverpool a poor lad to make my fortune. My mother was a decent woman, but my father was the greatest rip that ever walked on two feet.

"The poor woman took care that all my clothes were in good order, and she would not let me come to Liverpool unless I lodged with my employer.

"And you know what Brown? I did alright for myself. I worked my way up in that company through damned hard graft." There was a pause, before he barked out the word "graft" again bitterly.

"And the family must have thought something of me – for a few years later they let me marry the old man's daughter. How about that for a poor lad from Lancashire, eh?"

Williamson lowered himself tentatively onto a wooden beam that had been left on the lawn beside the hole. Brown sat down beside him. Both men sat for a moment considering the hole.

"I married Elizabeth, at St. Thomas' church on the twelfth day of December, in the year 1802." Williamson announced, his attention still fixedly on the hole, "I came out of that church door dressed in my hunting pink and went straight off and joined the hunt. And a damned fine hunt we had too.

"The following year this poor Lancashire lad had bought Tate's. I ran that business for fifteen year or more, and I made a considerable fortune for myself.

"I am no mug Brown. I know how to make money, and how to save money. But I also know poverty. I know what it is like to have that great demon of death licking at his lips and looking down on you feverishly.

"What I am trying to say Brown, is that those men will be paid until the day that great demon finally gets his hands on me. And until then he'll not get his hands on any of them or theirs.

"So be up early in the morning. It's going to take a lot of work to get that hole filled back in and have Miss Masons' lawn relayed."

***

The rain lashed down from the darkness upon the rocky slopes of Golgotha like a great demon of death licking at its lips.

Flashes of magnesium lightening crackled above the Gotterdammerung vision, as Williamson slipped across the mounds of scree behind his flickering eyelids.

The bodies hung limply from the splintered beams. And His blood-matted hair was caked across His face.

The armoured chest plate of the centurion rang out a flickering rattle as he gasped at the base of the cross.

Kneeling in the blood-soaked earth, and supporting his heavy body with the long wooden handle of his spear, he looked up towards the heavens, his face drowning in the lashing rain.

Williamson tripped and fell. He plunged his left hand out into the darkness to save himself.

But as he regained his composure he found that the palm of his hand had landed on the pointed crest of the rock, and a deep but painless seam opened in his palm. His blood oozed gently along the lines of his hand, and trickled across his wrist.

Lifted high on the breeze he watched the centurion slump prostrate before the executed. The hill vanished into the blackness and the bloody seeping scar he cradled in his palm began to churn with the iron-crested waves of the Mersey.

The angry river erupted in torrents of spray. Each deep-seated wave seemed to be desperately struggling against its neighbour.

Williamson watched as a cormorant stood defiant upon a crest of Golgotha, which peaked through the tumult. It looked up towards the heavens, wings out-stretched to dry, but its beaked face slowly drowning in the lashing rain.

In a single flap of its great wings it flew up through the darkness, thrust its wings straight back on its torpedo descent, pierced the angry waves and was gone.

Williamson followed the bird into the rock grey water and descended deep through the blinding silt.

And there deep beneath the shadowy cloak of the waves upon the cobbles of Wolstenhome Square, an urchin coughed out his final breaths – which showed themselves guiltily on ethereal wisps.

Williamson woke with such a start that he had thrown himself from his bed and was panting against the windowpane before he realised he was awake. His breath misted the window, and created patterns in the icy light of the moon.

The ancient church tower was silhouetted against the whiteness. Williamson looked upon it, and felt a realisation shudder through the passages of his brain.

The rain lashed down upon the old ashen tower like a great demon of death licking at its lips.

***

Williamson looked down upon the narrow muddy path that led from his garden gate to the churchyard.

The sun was edging its way from behind a cloud and puddles on the path sparkled like diamonds.

"Sundays are muddy days," Williamson said aloud. From the other side of the room Elizabeth chose to ignore him.

"Do you not think that the path to the church is a disgrace?"

"It is a nuisance," she confessed.

"It is a nuisance. It is," Williamson muttered thoughtfully. "In fact I think it is a disgrace. After all if we can't get to church without getting muddy, what does that say about us?"

"That we have a muddy path leading to the church?"

"Yes, but what would He make of it?"

"I am sure that He would be pleased to see us prepared to get muddy to go to church."

"Golgotha was thick with mud," Williamson said as he left the room.

Within days a group of thirty men had set to work on the path. They dug a deep trench the length of it, shoring up with timber as they went.

After weeks of digging and shoring, a group of masons set about building an intricate brick-arched roof across the span of the muddy gash.

Each morning Williamson looked down upon the developing structure with a smile, before announcing anew that "Gologotha was thick with mud."

Elizabeth grew more concerned about her husband. Elaborately wasting money by paying men to dig holes was reassuringly senseless. But this seemed frighteningly contrived.

By Easter the construction was complete. Steps, carved into the bedrock at the bottom of the garden led into the cool dark tunnel.

Williamson proudly led Elizabeth through the tunnel on Easter Sunday. The darkness was broken at regular intervals by flaming torches, and small bunches of spring flowers broke up the intricate lines of interlocking bricks.

The locals gathered at the church to see their eccentric neighbour christening his new structure – they were all smiles and cheers. All except one pair of old yellow eyes that watched carefully from the shadows.

Looking at the perfect span of herringbone brickwork Williamson allowed a tear of pride to secretly well. It was gone by the time he reached the light at the end of the tunnel.

Peaceful weeks passed by, without a single dream haunting Williamson's night. But one day as summer was breaking into the world, and the tunnel had become as normal and unnoticed as the handle on his bedroom door, he became sullen once more.

His men had gone back to building garden curios and useless arbours, and Williamson longed for the daily thrill of the tunnel project.

At night he became tormented once again by the sight of Christ upon the cross. He saw His eyes writhe grotesquely in the throes of suffocation, and heard his delicate lips emit the ghastly coughs of agony.

He prayed for hours at a time upon the icy stone floor of the dark and empty church, before wandering morosely home through the pitch-black world of the tunnel.

One day he walked through the tunnel, but did not enter the church. Instead he carried on along the muddy path that led him down to a sandstone cliff face and a quiet piece of scrubland.

Laying on the rocky ground with the gentle Mersey breeze playing across his sun-warmed face, he saw in the cliff a hollowed cove.

So slight was the indentation that he wondered whether it was only in his imagination. But staggering up to the rockface he could see that it was eroded a little. The sandstone glistened in the sun, its edges rounded like the creased rolls of fat on a baker's stomach.

Then it came to him. It came to him in a rush of thoughts – a barrage of images that shot through his head like blood in a dizzy spell.

To dig straight into the rock, he thought, would eventually lead beneath the church.

And if we carried on into the Earth, we would go directly beneath the house.

This was it. This was the tunnel that would outstretch the previous project. Longer and deeper, it was the light that Williamson had craved, and within hours the work had begun.

***

"We must undermine the very house of God itself," he told the foreman as he unveiled the elaborate blue prints, carefully drawn in his own hand.

The foreman nodded. He had grown accustomed to Williamson's eccentric plans, and lived gratefully through his working day, with the glassy expression that comes of unquestioning labour.

Williamson patted the man on the back, and left the room. He walked happily out of the building and into the sunshine. He wandered along the street and under the stone archway that led into the small communal garden that Williamson's men had built as part of an earlier project.

Sat on the lawn, with the plans opened on the grass in front of him, he was basking in the tranquillity of the moment when she appeared.

Her bonnet came into sight first, and then her shoulders and long red dress, as she walked over the grassy hill towards Williamson.

"Miss Henderson," Williamson said chirpily, tipping the rim of his hat.

"Mr Williamson, what a fine day we are enjoying," she smiled, with a gentle innocence.

"Indeed, indeed."

"Are these your latest plans?" she asked, peering over his shoulder. "May I look at them?"

"Yes," he smiled, handing them up through the sunbeams.

He studied her face as she studied the blueprints. She was young, he noticed for the first time. Younger than he had somehow believed. Her brow knotted gently, and her lips moved a little to silently shape the words on the page.

Her skin was pale and unblemished. It was satin across her dimpled cheeks, and ran smooth and clear as water down to her swan-like neck.

In a moment Williamson was uncontrollably young again, the years seemed to fall from him like leaves from an autumn branch.

"What do you think?" he asked.

"They are beautiful," she smiled, "Beautifully drawn on the page, I mean. Each brick so individual, it must have taken you hours."

"But what of the vision?" he asked, "What do you think of the idea?"

"I don't know."

"To undermine the church with a tunnel of this size, is it not wonderfully…" He struggled to find the word, "perfect?"

"Yes, Mr Williamson, in a curious way, it is beautiful."

Williamson struggled up from the ground, and wandered across the lawn with his new admirer.

A breeze blew across his old face.

"Thank you," he said, lifting the blueprints out of her hands, and walked away across the lawn. Her brow knotted once more, as her eyes followed him until he was gone.

***

The tunnel was completed by the middle of the summer. And a second and third were built at right angles across it for no other reason than a desire by Williamson to build the likeness of an Anglican cross beneath the church.

He chose not to tell the vicar, and this alone amused him for the best part of a decade. But an old unnoticed figure followed closely behind Williamson on his morning walks, a pair of glassy yellow eyes studying Williamson's stocky outline.

Feeling mysteriously uncomfortable, Williamson moved his daily saunter underground.

But he soon became bored by walking in the new tunnels, and focused the work of his men on a series of other, more sporadic constructions, which led out from the cross in haphazard fashion, based on Williamson's whims.

In less time than it takes the Mersey to cut a new headland into the red rocks of the Wirral peninsula, Williamson and his men had cut a maze of tunnels beneath the streets of Edge Hill.

Secret and seductive, they slowly became Williamson's private world. A place to retreat from the strains and disappointments of the world above.

Like the troglodytes of old, he would find refuge in the damp and bleeding rock – growing evermore contented in the half light and the putrid, stale air.

And when he became bored with building tunnels, Williamson would request a nook here, or a small subterranean room there.

One day, when Williamson was particularly bored by the singing of the birds in the trees of his garden, he asked the foreman to build him "something big".

"Something big, I say," he said. "A hall. A Great Hall. A Great Hall worthy of any castle or country home."

The foreman looked to the sky and made rabbits of the clouds as he listened.

Williamson followed his gaze with a smile – he saw the mainstays of Christ's cross where the foreman saw two long upright ears.

"I know that this is the right move to make," Williamson announced, somewhat dramatically, before moving back towards the house.

***

And so the masons chipped and chipped at the end of the tunnel for weeks. Williamson listened through the kitchen floorboards, and smiled.

His smile grew into a beam as the foreman unveiled the Great Hall – a long rectangular chasm deep below the hill.

Scores of tunnels pierced the walls of the underground room, and candles flickered from their positions wedged into the masonry, staining the walls with inky black shadows.

Williamson ordered the masons to carry down furniture from the dining room – rugs, the long oak table, even a chaise lounge.

And then it was complete. "A Great Hall fit for any castle," Williamson muttered, as he sat back in the high-winged leather chair and admired the work.

***

They all received an invitation - the great and the good from across Liverpool. Businessmen and shipping merchants, socialites and men of the cloth, friends and acquaintances from Williamson's former business life.

A great banquet in a Great Hall, the invitation boasted. So they came. All of them, buzzing with anticipation, wondering what the great man had built now.

"Folk have taken to calling him the King of Edge Hill," one elderly merchant gossiped through a thick white beard, as the throng gathered inside Williamson's home.

All across the room tongues lashed out words laced with rumour and tittle-tattle.

"His generosity is legendary," a bushy-eyebrowed banker whispered conspiratorially to a horse-like woman. "We're in for something of a treat, I'd warrant."

But when Williamson finally appeared in the doorway, he simply grinned like a shark, his head cocked to one side, and signalled for his guests to follow him towards the rear of the house.

He shuffled along through the backstair corridors, beyond the scullery, and through the oak and copper colours of the kitchen. The guests examined each others' faces quizzically, as if all the answers to their questions might be laying in their frowns.

Williamson finally stopped at the end of the darkest and dampest corridor in the building, and with a smile back towards his guests, he opened a heavy old oak door, to reveal a small whitewashed room.

The battered and sturdy, knife-marked kitchen table had been carried into the centre of the dimly lit room, and laid with spartan cutlery and coarse wooden goblets, where the guests had expected to find fine silver tableware and crystal wine glasses.

"Well come on in," Williamson muttered.

The bemused guests sat down on the painted wood and wickerwork chairs in silence.

The cook joined the two scullery maids to serve the guests with a plate of simple gruel, and a glass of dark ale. Incredulous frowns developed around the table.

Williamson sat back and watched his guests with a wry smile for half a minute, before the silence was shattered by the sound of a chair being pushed back against the coarse flagstones.

A middle-aged man, with an upturned nose kicked his chair back and walked out of the room, making a scoffing grunt. A few more moments passed before another man stood up, and taking his wife's arm, also left the room.

A flurry of silently disgruntled guests left the room. Williamson's expression remained as a static grin, until the final pair of stomping feet had gone. He then sat up in his chair, and looked around at the faces of the half a dozen guests that had remained at the table.

As they began to pick up spoons, and started tucking into their plates of gruel, Williamson stood up at the end of the table.

"Now I know who my real friends are," he announced in a formal voice. "So please, friends come and join me for that feast I promised you."

And leading the way back out into the corridor, Williamson took them to a small archway at the end of the passage, and down a steep flight of steps. The guests examined each other's puzzled frowns all over again.

"Now he's taking us to the cellar," an old vicar whispered to Miss Henderson, who was lagging behind at the back of the line.

But the steps seemed to go on and on – beyond the depth of any normal cellar, and when they finally reached the bottom of the steps, the group found themselves in a long, straight tunnel of herringbone brickwork.

At the end of the tunnel the guests descended another staircase, and Emily Henderson smiled knowingly, as the group looked upon the Great Hall – resplendent with chandeliers and leather armchairs, it stretched for almost 100ft into the darkness beyond.

And in the centre of the gilded room a long polished mahogany table stood proudly, bearing a dreamlike feast, with crystal and silverware shining finely in the candlelight.

"Come on my friends," Williamson chuckled. "Let's eat."

***

Merry with the velvet taste of brandy still on his lips, Williamson had waved goodbye to his guests.

For a moment he thought he caught sight of a pair of old yellow eyes in the shadows across the street, but with a second glance they were gone.

Closing the great oak door on the world, he shuffled up to his bedroom, and slumped down on to the bed fully dressed – his muddy shoes trailing damp stains across the sheets.

But as his eyes slowly closed upon the darkness of the room, Williamson became aware of a voice. It pleaded in angry sobs, but Williamson couldn't quite hear what the pleas were for.

Then a world opened up before Williamson's dreaming eyes. He was back again on the hill outside the high walls of Jerusalem.

As the wind and rain lashed across the landscape, Williamson's gaze drew up the twisted rough wood of the central cross.

He saw again the blood-stained feet, over-crossed and pinned against the wood by a brutal nail.

He looked up across the writhing muscles of the body, twitching and arched, almost lifeless in their grotesque rippling pulsation – like a dead fish being moved across the seabed by the current.

Then Williamson finally looked at the face, slumped down now, resting upon the still tense shoulder.

He looked at the features of the face – deep-set and dark, but frowning and pained, not the peaceful expression of the Son of God that Williamson had seen so many times above the altar of his church.

But as he looked closer at the face the world melted around him. He heard the sound of boots walking across wooden floorboards.

The body still hung rigidly from the cross, but now it stood inside a long, oak-panelled room.

Then the figure on the cross changed. The beard was gone. The dark, deep-set features of the face were lifted in terror, and a pair of bright blue eyes were pleading desperately.

Two men stood at the base of the cross, watching the struggle without expression.

"I am innocent of these deeds father," the anguished voice cried out across the room, before adding with a sob, "Father, why hast thou forsaken me?"

But as Williamson's slumbering face twisted into a frown, the room around the cross disappeared.

And finally the cross itself seemed to fall limply towards Williamson, turning grey and watery, before it finally broke into a wave.

Soon it was surrounded by a thousand more waves, stretching out into the mist. At the horizon Williamson could just make out the arching strip of land on the other side of the Mersey.

The wind and the rain lashed against his face. And as the gusts blew harder they picked up the veneer of the crests of each of the thousands of grey waves.

The water mingled with the rain as it filtered through the wrinkles and crevasses of Williamson's old face, and left a taste of salt upon his lips.

Violently he threw himself upright in his bed. Bright sunshine filtered through the gap in the curtains, and Williamson still had the velvet taste of brandy in his mouth.

***

Elizabeth died on a cold day in March, 1822. Her departure was swift and uncomplicated.

Williamson had started the day in high spirits, tinkering in the garden. He was building a rockery for his wife – she had seen one on a visit to a friend's house, and had talked of little else since.

It was to be a surprise for her, and Williamson had worked in the freezing temperatures before dawn, to create the offering before she had even woken.

But Elizabeth never woke that morning. And when Williamson bounded into her room shortly before 10 o'clock, an excited smile on his face, she lay still beneath her covers.

Her pale, lifeless face looked 20 years younger in death. And Williamson's smile remained fixed as the tears quietly negotiated the crevasses and lines of his cheeks.

Folk said he would follow her – wouldn't survive without her. But life doesn't always fall like romantic fiction, and he just lived on.

He mourned for months. Quiet in public, and desperate when alone. His sobs would take him through sleepless nights, and his watery eyes would lead him through the empty days.

But little changed. His men continued to work. Williamson had threatened to sack any one who stopped working as a mark of respect during her funeral. So they carried on, never stopping, never showing the old man the sympathy he didn't want to see.

The months turned into years, and Williamson could go for days without a thought to his wife. Then he would endure the guilt of having gone so long immune to her loss.

He dreamed of nothing through those years. But would wake in the night in a panic – suddenly unable to remember her voice or the colour of her eyes.

"I was sorry to part with the old girl when she went," he admitted one night to the foreman as they drank together.

"We led a cat and dog life of it for the most part, it's true," he added with a smile. "But the world seems quiet without her."

***

Edge Hill didn't stay quiet for long.

Williamson's loss was overwhelmed by the appearance of a subterranean rival - an engineer called George Stephenson had also taken to carving up the hillside.

And the hundreds of Irish navvies the young man brought with him, made rapid progress as they cut an 80ft deep, 20ft wide swathe into the heart of Williamson's underground territory.

"They are going to lay a line of tracks to run a steam engine between Liverpool and Manchester," Williamson explained to a bemused-looking Emily Henderson, as they stood together, watching the canyon-like gape develop before them.

"By cutting down like this, they will be able to avoid the hill almost entirely," he went on, clearly impressed by the tenacity of his rival.

Williamson could see nothing but masons at work, and carpenters shoring the rocks around them with gargantuan wooden frames. He watched with childlike enthusiasm.

Within an hour he had called all his men around him.

"If any one of you can get work from Stephenson, for this magnificent project, then you must take it," he bellowed.

"I will feel no sense of betrayal, and I will welcome each one of you back when the job is done. I would only ask that no word of our work here gets back to Mr Stephenson."

But their enquiries with Stephenson all proved fruitless. He had his workers, and knew nothing of these men or their work beneath Edge Hill.

So the legions of Irish navvies worked away through the day and night, completely unaware of Williamson's men, who tunnelled through the rock around them – often reaching just feet from each others' chisels.

But one day, as the summer sun lingered lazily over the evening scene, Williamson wandered across his garden, and into the house through the back door. Stepping lightly across the kitchen, he opened the door to the cellar, and walked down the steep, twisting steps.

Far away, through the grimy labyrinth, his workers were busy in staccato candlelight. Masons, with concentrated frowns focused on the elaborate herringbone pattern brick archway, which was extended ever deeper into the earth.

The diggers and the labourers scraped ever deeper into the sand-coloured rock, and a grumbling carpenter was shoring-up the excavation with heavy oak beams.

Williamson smiled broadly as he arrived at the scene, and signalled for the men to carry on.

He watched the work develop for a while, sat back on an abandoned pile of shoring timber.

As he surveyed the scene he reached into his waistcoat pocket and pulled out a small pipe.

He tapped it against the timber to empty the barrel, before nimbly filling it with fresh tobacco, and lighting it with a match.

Williamson puffed luxuriously on the pipe, and sent a faint cloud of smoke, and a strong smell of leafy tobacco through the tunnel.

Half an hour later, he tapped his pipe against the timber once again to clean it out. Tap, tap, tap – the hollow sound echoed even above the sound of the workers.

Tap, tap, tap. He brushed out the remaining leaves with a swipe of his index finger into the barrel. Tap, tap, tap. The noise came again, but this time the pipe was firmly held in Williamson's hand, away from the timber.

Williamson looked at the pipe barrel, with confusion.

"Quiet a moment," he bellowed to the workers, who stopped their toil in a frozen tableau of the scene.

Tap, tap, tap. There it was again. The men frowned at each other, curiously looking around the tunnel for the culprit.

Tap, tap, tap. It was getting louder, and each tap was followed by a rocky scraping noise.

Williamson got to his feet and walked towards the excavated rock face. He placed his ear to the wall. "It's them," he muttered. "It's Stephenson's men." The noise grew louder again.

"Gentlemen," he whispered. "I believe we could have a little fun here of our own."

The workers looked at him blankly.

"Fun and games, my boys, fun and games."

Williamson looked around quizzically.

"You boy," he said to the youngest of the puzzled workers. "Run back up and fetch two tins of the red brick paint, and the rest of you, strip to your waists."

Obediently the men took off their jackets and shirts, as the crack of the pick-axe edged ever closer to their tunnel.

***

Within the hour three dozen Irish navvies were to be seen running as fast as their legs could carry them out of Stephenson's great tunnel. They ran past Stephenson, and on into the streets of the city, disappearing like as many terrified mice into the bustling crowds of Lime Street.

Baffled, the great engineer held on to the foreman's collar, as he also tried to flee from the tunnel entrance.

"We dug ourselves all the way to hell itself," he blubbered in his heavy Irish accent, tears welling in his eyes, and panic painted across his face. "And as we cut tru dat final rock between our world and Satan's, der he was, the divil himself, surrounded as he was sir by a multitude of demons."

And as Stephenson burst into laughter, the navvy freed himself from his master's clutch, and fled towards the docks.

The following day Williamson's men found themselves with a new master, for a few months at least.

***

Richard fumbled inside his pocket, and picked out the box of matches. He pushed his finger into the side of the box, only to hear them scatter delicately into the darkness.

As he fumbled around on his hands and knees trying to feel for a match he also dropped the lamp. It crashed on the steps two or three times, and landed with a distant thud.

Richard felt about the cold steps blindly. He talked frantically to himself.

As he fumbled his foot slipped and he fell down three or four of the steps before stopping his fall by clawing at the central spire of rock.

He lay in the darkness for a moment on his back, wet now, and shivering.

The only other sound he could hear was the distant dripping of water in the banqueting hall below.

Eventually Richard discovered a match on the ground. He struck it against the rock. For a moment the staircase spiralled up before him, and then dimmed once more as the flame died.

Richard found another match, but it was damp, and wouldn't strike at all.

Panic rose up through his throat like a flame. He gasped, and stumbled. On his hands and knees, he began to climb.

He seemed to be climbing for a long time before he reached the top. The ground below him flattened out, and looking up he could see a sharp beam of light filtering down into the darkness.

He tripped and stumbled in the direction of the shaft of light, which grew brighter as he progressed towards it.

Reaching the end of the passageway, he fell down a couple of steps, wincing as a sharp pain stung his ankle. He was in a small room. There was a cold fireplace cut out of the rock, and the shaft of light beamed down the chimney.

Dimly lit, the room took shape before his eyes. There was a small rough-cut wooden table, strewn across with papers. There stood a brass oil lamp, dark now, but soot-stained from use.

Then he was struck by an overpowering smell. It seemed to punch him in the face with its torrid stench.

Stumbling backwards he made out another shape. Beside the fireplace there was a large chair, and slowly the slumped silhouette of a chubby man began to emerge as Richard's eyes adjusted to the light.

Tentatively he stepped towards it. As he did so the light from the chimney swelled, and there before him sat the molten corpse of a once great man.

***

Williamson slept soundly for weeks, content by day to watch his workers progress on Stephenson's network.

But when the project was nearing completion, one by one he took his men back to his own subterranean works.

And the dreams came back to haunt his nights. He saw Him hanging limply on the cross. Some nights would pass entirely with Williamson forced to watch the nails being hammered into those holy hands time after time after time.

In church each Sunday Williamson would be joined by the old retired vicar of the parish – a near-blind man in his 90s, who rarely spoke, but followed Williamson out of church with a shuffle.

And, Williamson fancied, the old clergyman watched him from the church door, as he took his morning walk each day. He knew the old man couldn't see more than a few feet. He could see only God in front of his eyes, yet his head moved to follow Williamson's figure on the brow of that distant hill.

But one Sunday the old minister finally spoke. Before the weekly church service, he joined Williamson, sitting closely beside him in the pew.

"You're seeing him, aren't you?" the old man whispered, through his flushed-white lips. "I can tell," he added. "I've been concerned for you."

Williamson looked at the old man, his bleached skin taut like a dead man's across his face, his yellow eyes piercing the withered old face to look straight at him.

"I see him too," he said slowly. "I see lots of things." He paused to look over his shoulder, before adding: "I speak to them you know? Those who came before."

Williamson frowned. "I don't understand, sir," he muttered.

"Two centuries ago there stood a house on this hill, where holy men lived," the old man said. "A kind of seminary, the puritans ran for their ministers. But one young priest they suspected of evil," he paused, looked around him again, and in even more hushed tones added, "evil sir, with another man."

"I don't understand," Williamson repeated.

"They punished him you see, but I think he was innocent of their charges," the old clergyman went on. "But know you how they punished him?"

Williamson shook his head.

"They gave him a death to match the Lord's own sufferings, sir." The old man stopped to give a loud phlegm-filled cough. "They crucified him you see," he added, as he regained his composure. "They nailed him to a cross right there in their dining hall, and watched him…"

But before he could finish his sentence, the organ piped-up, and with the start of the service, the old man would speak no more.

***

In the weeks that followed Williamson could think of little else. The thought of a latter day crucifixion filled him with horror by day, and the scene played out time and again to haunt his sleep.

Finally, waking amid his sweat soaked sheets, Williamson gave a pitiful whimper, and hurriedly dressed.

He found the old clergyman in prayer at the front of the church, and sitting down beside him, he whispered: "What can I do for him?"

The minister opened his cloudy eyes mid-prayer, and turned to Williamson.

"You can pray for him," he said. "His tormented soul permeates the very fabric of this whole hillside," he added quietly. "It is his will that makes you undermine Edge Hill with your tunnels isn't it?"

Williamson met the question with stony-faced silence.

"He comes to you at night, doesn't he?" The old man added.

Williamson looked to the ground. "The tunnels are merely a rouse," he said at last. "An occupation for the work-less."

"Maybe after the wars," the old man chuckled. "But not now. It's more than that. It's in your soul."

Williamson looked to the ground once more.

"I may be able to help you," the old minister added. "If I can only find the strength." He stopped to think for a moment. "If I could be strong enough, I might try exorcising the hill."

"What could he do to you?" Williamson asked.

"I mean only to help him," he added. "I mean to help him move over to the light," and with a smile he revealed his bleached gums. "But he may not be fond of men of the cloth."

***

Within a week the old man was ready to begin, and Williamson had sent all his men home on full pay. The labyrinth of damp tunnels beneath Edge Hill were silent, and empty.

"I must pray a while," the elderly minister said, closing the church doors upon Williamson.

As he did so the distant sound of thunder echoed across the sky, and Williamson felt the first large heavy raindrops fall upon his face.

The old man's prayers went on for the whole day, and the torrential rain flowed from the sky for as long as his prayers ran up in the opposite direction.

Eventually Williamson went home to bed, leaving the old minister in the church. The rain still fell through the whole of the next day, and an impatient Williamson strode up and down in the churchyard.

Only occasionally, when lightening sheeted across the charcoal sky, could Williamson make out the black silhouette of the old man in prayer through the stained-glass windows of the church.

By the third day Williamson had given up hope on the project, and sat sullenly in his kitchen, looking at the doorway into the tunnels, which were all the while filling with the mounting rainwater which seemed never to stop falling from the sky.

Emily Henderson watched over Williamson, convinced he must be sickening, but he refused to speak to her.

At last on the fifth day, the old minister emerged from the church. He was clearly weakened, and could barely walk as he made his way into Williamson's house.

"Lead me down," he muttered, and Williamson opened the door to reveal the subterranean staircase, heading down into the darkness.

Williamson helped the old man through the tunnels, with only a lantern to guide them.

"We must walk on," the clergyman muttered. "I will know the place."

At last, in Williamson's own underground Great Hall, the old man stopped, and began his service.

The rain washed down the walls of the cavern, as the weakened old man raised his voice. He held his bible aloft, knowing the psalms well enough to not need the holy book for anything other than comfort.

As his words echoed around the room, a great thudding began. It was distant at first, but with each moment the thudding grew louder and louder – as if giant fists were thudding on the very walls of the cavern.

***

Emily Henderson rushed into the kitchen, and seeing the tunnel door wide open, she ran down the staircase.

"Mr Williamson!" she shouted breathlessly into the darkness, and without a lamp, ran straight into the inky cloak of the tunnels.

***

Deep down in the Great Hall Williamson shielded his eyes in horror, as the furniture began to rumble, then shake, and finally throw itself angrily around the room.

But still the old man went on, his hands now aloft, and his words chuntering mantra-like from his lips.

The veins pulsed through the tracing paper skin of his temples.

Williamson retreated to the corner of the room, his own heart racing, while the old man dropped suddenly to his knees and omitted the longest outpouring of breath Williamson had ever heard.

It gurgled through the foaming saliva on his pallid lips, and rattled from the deepest recesses of his throat. Yet still the furniture continued to shudder, and lamps and chairs and gaming tables thrust themselves violently from wall to wall.

Williamson was himself thrown back against the rock face with a violent thrust to his chest. He thought for a moment he was being pinned against the wall by an angry bookcase or a demonic drinks cabinet. But as he lowered his eyes to his chest, there was no furniture against him, yet still the crushing came.

Desperate to retreat, he scurried towards the rough-cut stairs on the far side of the room. The pain was moving through his body now, and Williamson clawed at the biceps of his left arm as he ran away.

A woman's scream could be heard in the distance echoing through the brickwork intestines of the labyrinth.

***

Emily Henderson was now completely enveloped by the darkness, and the rain water rushed down from the ceiling, and ran across her terrified body.

With no real sense of direction in that pitch-black night, she stumbled on, hearing the tumult grow louder along the tunnel.

Then in a breathless moment, she felt as her feet slid frantically along the wet floor, until they were met with empty air beneath them. And there was nothing but falling in her final seconds.

***

Williamson made it to the room at the top of the stairs, and collapsed into his armchair. The sweat ran in streams down his face, as he stared towards the ceiling. From within the knotted rock, he believed for a moment that he saw a face.

It smiled down upon him in a sort of knowing way. He saw the mouth, and the worn, unkempt ragged beard and the once angry, now resigned eyes of a man lost to his cause.

The rock stood before him now like a man, and beckoned slowly. Williamson followed.

Saint Peter's hands were rugged and brown. Not the hands of a tax collector at all, but in the dewy brown eyes of the Galilean, Williamson could see the reflection of Our Lord upon the cross, in the agony of crucifixion.

The wound across his ribcage wept, and his crippled arms shook violently at the shoulders. His feet were torn through, and there was terror in His eyes.

The vomiting had stopped. The bleeding had waned. And now the sky erupted with rain, and to the lightening-strewn night he raised his thorny head in a final twisted flail and asked in a long forgotten tongue, "Father, why hast thou forsaken me?"

His beard then fell upon his chest, and the bloodied cry of hopelessness ebbed into the wretched night upon the barren hillside.

From a view across the ancient streets of Jerusalem, and surrounded by the lifeless hanging bodies of thieves, he closed his eyes upon the world for the final time.

Distant in the night sky, high above, Williamson followed a light across Gethsemane, where he saw from the edge of a void the brightly lit clock face reflecting upon the granite waves.

Watching over time itself he saw the winged figures of Griffin-like creatures, talons clinging delicately to hope.

He saw buildings of the future and of the past, and upon the Mersey the bloodied scent of human cargo.

Shielding his eyes from the cries of young boys in chains, he watched in horror the line of men trudge across the battle-torn plains of France.

Walking home in weariness and finding Liverpool a fate worse than death – where depression ebbed across the diseased streets.

Where children died hungry and naked and without a cross, but with only agony and suffering and hopelessness.

And there beneath the shadowy cloak of night upon the cobbles of Wolstenhome Square, an urchin coughed out his final breaths – which showed themselves guiltily on ethereal wisps.

The vomiting had stopped. The bleeding had waned. And now the sky erupted with rain, and to the thunder lighted night he raised his tiny head in a final twisted flail and asked in a guttural dockside accent, "Father, why hast thou forsaken me?"

From a view across the port's ancient streets, and surrounded by the lifeless slumped bodies of thieves, he closed his eyes upon the world for the final time.

And in the knotted rocky beams, among his swirling wretched dreams, Williamson saw Saint Peter cry, across the inky charcoal sky.

The World Of Williamson's Tunnels

The World Of Williamson's Tunnels:

A History Of The Mole Of Edge Hill

The Liverpool district of Edge Hill, little more than a mile out of the city centre is a fairly nondescript sort of a place today. Its residents go about their business in the cheerless setting of urban sprawl.

Surprisingly few among them know of the curious events that occurred here more than one hundred and fifty years ago, or of the great character who instigated them.

Yet the evidence of these strange times still exists today directly beneath their feet. For it was here that Edge Hill's most eccentric resident, Joseph Williamson, produced his most eccentric creation – a great subterranean labyrinth, which undermines so much of this rocky outcrop.

In this work I hope to explore the eccentric life and works of this singular character, and the way in which this 'eccentricity' has been both interpreted and constructed by writers and historians in the century and a half since his death.

The tunnels have fallen into the realm of Liverpool folklore, with very little objective research from purely primary resources being carried out into them, but a great many myths and legends forming around these mysterious caverns.

Consequently today the line between fact and fiction is obscured, particularly as the majority of documentation on the tunnels is anecdotal. It is therefore my intention to both highlight the actual history of Williamson's tunnels, but also to document the history of the folklore and mythology which has established itself around them.

Joseph Williamson was born into poverty on the March 10, 1769 in the Lancashire town of Warrington. Little is known of the first decade of his life, however at the tender age of eleven he was sent to Liverpool to earn a living.

Williamson obtained a junior position in a tobacco company on Wolstenholme Square, owned by Richard Tate, and his son Thomas Moss Tate. He is said to have later recalled that:

> I came to Liverpool a poor lad to make my fortune. My mother was a decent woman, but my father was the greatest rip that ever walked on two feet. The poor woman took care that all my clothes were in good order, and she would not let me come to Liverpool unless I lodged with my employer. [1]

The self-conscious recollections by Williamson of his humble beginnings seem significant as the origin of the myth of the self-made man that now surrounds his image within the popular consciousness of local historians and their readers.

Similarly it seems to be largely the supposed quotes from Williamson himself which also go on to begin the presentation of him as an 'eccentric' in later life.

This sort of construction of a public identity is discussed by Jean Peneff in the essay *Myths in Life Stories*, in connection to a rapidly developing society, such as England in the first half of the nineteenth century:

> The mythical element in life stories is the pre-established framework within which individuals

---

[1] Williamson, J.; quote taken from Stonehouse, J.; *Recollections of Old Liverpool* (1863), J.F. Hughes Books (Liverpool), p170.

explain their personal history: the mental construct which, starting from the memory of individual facts which would otherwise appear incoherent and arbitrary, goes on to arrange and interpret them and so turn them into biographical events. Such mythical frameworks are common in all societies. They are especially widespread in societies undergoing rapid development and change, where individuals tell their histories as a kind of progress or journey.[2]

The young Williamson's journey saw him make considerably rapid progress – he obviously proved popular with his employer as over the next twenty years he progressed through the firm, and even married the boss's daughter, Elizabeth Tate, at St. Thomas' church on December 12, 1802.

The wedding day brought about the first recorded example of Williamson's eccentricity.

Williamson is said to have enjoyed hunting, and it was his bride's misfortune that their wedding day happened to occur on the same day as the popular Liverpool Hunt.

He arrived at the church wearing hunting-pink and throughout the ceremony had his hunter and groom waiting for him at the church door, so that he could make a rapid exit once the formalities were over, and rejoin the hunt.

The following year saw Williamson actually buy the Tate tobacco business from his new brother-in-law Thomas Moss Tate, who had himself succeeded ownership of the company after his father's death in 1787.

Williamson ran the business for the next fifteen years with great ingenuity, and made a considerable fortune. This 'rags to riches'

---

[2] Peneff, J.; 'Myths in Life Stories' (1990) in *The Myths We Live By* (1990), Routledge (London), p36.

story seems central to an interest being taken in Williamson after his death, especially by the Victorian historians, irrespective of his later eccentricities. Jean Peneff pays much attention to the mythological element in the biographies of 'the self-made man', and claims that a 'classic example'[3] of biographical mythology is:

> ...that of the dynamic entrepreneur who started out with nothing: the self-made man. Historians of capitalism such as Fernand Braudel, Sigmund Diamond, or Louis Bergeron, see this as almost a fiction. But the transformation of businessmen into industrial worthies, who started out with nothing or owe nothing to anyone, confers a favourable label on the whole business sector of capitalism.[4]

In his work of 1879 entitled *The Streets of Liverpool*, the Victorian historian James Stonehouse attempts to trace Williamson's 'rags to riches' story by claiming that:

> It has been said that from some information he obtained from General Gascoigne, connected with the tobacco trade, he cleared an immense amount of money.[5]

It is not known to what information Stonehouse is referring, but it does underline the clear fact that Williamson was both a shrewd and adept businessman, and also illustrates Stonehouse's fascination with the mysterious manner of Williamson's rise to success.

In 1806 however Williamson invested some money in purchasing an area of land around Mason Street, in the village of Edge Hill, then on the outskirts of Liverpool.

---

[3] Peneff, J.; *op.cit.*, p36.
[4] *ibid.*
[5] Stonehouse, J.; *The Streets of Liverpool* (1879), Edward Howell Co. (Liverpool), p132.

By 1818, as he approached his fiftieth birthday, Williamson evidently felt that it was time to begin spending his great fortune, and so retired from the tobacco industry to live at Edge Hill. It is fair to say though, that this merely marked the beginning of his life's work.

Williamson's property at Edge Hill consisted of a few acres of barren wasteland set upon the sandstone escarpment overlooking Liverpool.

It stretched from Miss Mason's property (after whose father the street was named in the previous century) in the north, to Grinfield Street in the south, and from Mason Street at its eastern-most border to Smithdown Lane in the West.

Williamson evidently saw the potential that the area had as a site for the construction of housing for the middle class – among whom it was commonly agreed that the air around Edge Hill was good for the constitution.

The country at this time was suffering from a great depression following the end of the Napoleonic wars, and Williamson, upon seeing the poverty of the local men, decided to employ them in his construction of houses on Mason Street.

Upon the completion of this practical work however Williamson did not cease to employ them, ever one to pity those in a less fortunate situation than himself.

He made little of his kindness, by stating that his motive in employing them was, '…if you give them something to do, no matter what, it keeps them out of mischief.'[6]

However this in many ways can be seen as the first job creation scheme. Out of purely philanthropic motives he would pay his men

---

[6] Williamson, J.; quote taken from Whale, D.; *Lost Villages of Liverpool - Part 2* (1984), Stephenson & Son (Liverpool), p41.

for the most pointless tasks. There are numerous tales of his paying a decent wage for men to dig holes, and refill them, or to pump water for hours, only to let it run away. One man was employed in moving a heap of stones from one place to another, only to be told to move them all back again.

Stonehouse recalls how when this man remonstrated with his employer for the pointlessness of his labour, Williamson replied:

> Now look here, look here, my man, I suppose your missus on Saturday night wants some money to go to market with, and if you get it for her, I don't suppose that either of you need care how you earn it, so that you do so honestly - wheel those stones back again.[7]

Williamson could not abide the idea of simply donating his money to charity, as he believed that working for a wage retained the men's self-respect.

On one occasion he was invited to sit on a Poor Aid Committee at St. Mary's church, along with other wealthy members of the community to discuss how they could best help the poor.

This was a subject often addressed during this period, particularly following the Royal Commission into the Poor Laws in 1832,[8] and the subsequent Poor Law Amendment Act of 1834.[9] The general debate of this period over the poor is summarised well by Ursula R. Q. Henriques in her work *Before the Welfare State: Social Administration in Early Industrial Britain* (1979), in which she explains that:

---

[7] Williamson, J.; quote taken from Stonehouse, J.; *The Streets of Liverpool* (1879), p135.
[8] The Royal Commission into the Poor Laws is addressed in some detail by Ursula R. Q. Henriques in *Before the Welfare State: Social Administration in Early Industrial Britain* (1979), Longman Ltd. (London), p26.
[9] Rayner, R.M.; *A History of England* (1933), Longmans, Green and Co. (London), p258.

> ... there were those who believed in the duty of the privileged to look after the unprivileged, and there were those who saw destitution as a consequence of if not a punishment for personal and social inadequacies.[10]

She goes on to explain that the influence of the first, philanthropic attitude was also counterbalanced by a fear that the poor would not work if they felt that they would never be allowed to become destitute.[11]

Williamson himself soon became irritated by the means of charity being suggested by the committee, and so turned to a Mr. Barker, the incumbent of St. Mary's and chairman of the meeting, and asked him how many men he employed. Mr. Barker replied that he employed none.

Williamson went around the table and asked each person present the same question, and they all had to admit that they did not employ any people apart from perhaps a house servant. Williamson stood up and asked the committee to follow him outside, where he showed them at least fifty men working for him on his land, and advised them all to do likewise and actually give the poor employment. The committee however just looked on aghast as they watched these men unnecessarily turning grindstones, digging holes and other such apparently pointless tasks.

Not all of Williamson's employment was completely pointless however, and upon completing his first houses on Mason Street he decided that they would benefit from having a garden at the rear.

However the land behind the houses sloped too dramatically. His ever-ingenious solution to this problem was to build raised gardens supported by a series of arches. This proved a great success,

---

[10] Henriques, U. R. Q.; *Before the Welfare State: Social Administration in Early Industrial Britain* (1979), p22.
[11] *ibid.*, p23.

but left a cavernous gorge beneath at the base of the sandstone hill. It was arguably this creation that first sparked his imagination to leanings of a subterranean nature.

As work on the houses was completed, and never able to render his men unemployed, he would order them to further excavate this cavern deeper into the sandstone cliff-face.

Gradually, what began as little more than a cave became a tunnel, and as work progressed under the ever-increasing influence of Williamson's imagination a veritable labyrinth developed under the streets of Edge Hill.

Williamson was undoubtedly a man of great character as well as imagination. There are many tales about his uncompromising acts, which are highly useful in creating a picture of his complex and colourful personality.

As the events of his wedding day perhaps should have indicated, his marriage with Elizabeth was famously turbulent, and arguing and bickering seem to have been a way of life for this unlikely couple.

This tension erupted most spectacularly when Williamson left the house in a rage and flung open the doors to his wife's aviary, exclaiming bitterly as the birds escaped:

> There! See how the poor devils like to get free. Many a married man would like to have wings and the doors of wedlock thrown open so that they might fly away and be at rest![12]

Despite their stormy relationship however, after his wife's death in 1822 Williamson is said to have admitted that, '…Betty and I lived but a cat and dog life of it, but I was sorry to part with the old

---

[12] *ibid.*, p138.

girl when she did go.'[13] In typical down-to-earth fashion he is said to have reprimanded his workers for ceasing work out of respect for his wife's funeral, telling them that, '…you work for the living, not for the dead. If you chaps don't turn to directly, I shall stop a day's wages on Saturday.' [14]

Williamson, while being firm with his employees, was also particularly kind to them, and regularly called his entire workforce together to give them a drink of ale or porter. Although they would usually get through a half-barrel on each occasion Williamson would merely remark that, '…they worked all the better for their throats being wetted.'[15]

This famous generosity was not confined to those whom he employed. On one occasion he is said to have invited a number of local distinguished gentlemen to dine with him. Upon arriving at his home on Mason Street they were shocked to be seated at a very basic table in a poorly furnished room.

Williamson sat at the head of the table and removed the lid from a tureen containing simple porridge, which was to be their meal. A number of the guests took offence at this treatment and left the house immediately.

Williamson courteously saw them to the door, before returning to those guests who had remained, telling them, 'Now that I know who really are my friends, pray follow me upstairs.'[16]

Needless to say, here they were greeted with the most generous and lavish meal in a richly furnished dining room.

---

[13] Williamson, J.; quote taken from Stonehouse, J.; *Recollections of Old Liverpool* (1863), p170.
[14] *ibid.,* p171.
[15] Williamson, J.; quote taken from Stonehouse, J.; *The Streets of Liverpool* (1879), p140.
[16] Williamson, J.; quote taken from Whittington-Egan, R.; *Liverpool Characters and Eccentrics* (1985), Gallery Press (Wirral), p11.

Williamson was the sort of landlord who would quite happily and very generously spend enormous amounts of money in improving his houses, if he happened to like the tenants that lived in them.

In a paper made for the Historic Society of Lancashire and Cheshire in 1858, entitled *The Excavations at Edge Hill, With a Brief Notice of the Late Joseph Williamson*, James Stonehouse recalls speaking to a lady who had moved to the area in 1838.[17]

She was engaged in looking for suitable accommodation for her family when she was advised to approach Williamson, whose houses seemed an ideal size. She was also particularly keen to rent a house on Mason Street as her doctor had recommended the air of Edge Hill.

Upon approaching Williamson she received a coldly disinterested response at first. However after a while he asked her what sort of house she wanted. Her response, which proved a great amusement to Williamson, was simply, 'Why, one with three parlours, six bedrooms, and every convenience'.[18]

He then sneeringly went on to ask her what she was willing to pay for her accommodation. Telling him that she could pay thirty pounds a year amused Williamson further, who sarcastically called his workmen around him and asked them if they had ever heard such nonsense. After the required response of a loyal sneer, and hearty agreement with their master, they were sent back to work.

Once they had gone Williamson stood silently thinking for a couple of minutes, before asking the lady and her friend (who had accompanied her for moral support – knowing of Williamson's peculiarities) to follow him to a house in Mason Street that he felt

---

[17] Stonehouse, J.; 'The Excavations at Edge Hill, with a Brief Notice of the Late Joseph Williamson' (1858) in *Transactions of the Historic Society of Lancashire and Cheshire* (1917) Volume 68, R. & R. Clark Ltd. (Edinburgh), p16.
[18] *ibid.*, p17.

could be suitable. They did so, but the lady felt that she would prefer a house with smaller rooms but more of them.

Williamson listened to her, and asked her to return on the following Thursday. Upon doing so she found that Williamson had completely gutted and refitted the entire house so as to make the accommodation exactly as she had required. Her new landlord then went on to insist upon charging a rent much less than she had previously agreed. He later admitted to having taken to the lady because of the way in which she had stood up to him in the street.

However Stonehouse actually refers to her as 'a lady of some personal attractions',[19] and it might be a reasonable assumption that Williamson was also taken with her looks – especially as we are given to understand that Williamson later referred to her as 'the Queen of Edge Hill'.[20] This was a reference to Williamson's own popular title of 'the King of Edge Hill' – given to him by the locals because of his philanthropic employment of the poor.

A few years later the lady, whose new home neighboured Williamson's own home, decided that as her family was growing she needed more nursery space.

She asked her landlord neighbour if he could attend to it, as he might as well be spending his money on building something useful – rather than working on his apparently useless caverns and tunnels. However his response was simply, '…not for £30 a year!'[21]

In a last effort she wrote to her neighbour entreating the King of Edge Hill to build the nursery for his Queen. A few mornings later, as she washed her baby, she received a gracious reply from him using similar rhetoric. As she later recalled she had no sooner finished reading the letter, and returned to washing her child when:

---

[19] *ibid.,* p16.
[20] *ibid.*
[21] *ibid.,* p18.

> ...I heard a tremendous knocking at the side of the wall nearest to me. Presently portions of plaster fell down, and to my consternation and astonishment a portion of the brickwork was removed, and an opening made into my chamber.[22]

She goes on to explain that no sooner had the hole appeared in the wall than Williamson stepped in out of the cloud of dust. As he heartily explained that he had a room for her nursery a group of his workmen scurried around, fitting a doorframe and repairing the wall around it.

When she was then led through this new door by her landlord, in a state of shock and covered in dust and plaster, she discovered that he had given up the thirty foot long drawing room of his own house for the purpose.

This particular example of his generosity is probably also due in part to the fact that he had a great fondness for children, and a great regret that he had never fathered any of his own.

Stonehouse claims that Williamson was known to have said of them, 'Ah, there's no deceit in children. If I had had some, I should not have been the arch-rogue I am.'[23]

However Stonehouse generally seems to be concerned with the construction of Williamson as a heart-warming, loveable character – and this quotation probably says more about Stonehouse's motives in his historicisation of Williamson, than it actually does about Williamson himself.

It does seem however that Williamson's sense of humour enjoyed surprising people such as he did in installing the nursery.

---

[22] *ibid.*, p18.
[23] Williamson, J.; quote taken from Stonehouse, J.; *Recollections of Old Liverpool* (1863), p172.

On another occasion one of his tenants reported that their house was damp. A few days later, early in the morning a servant in the house was lighting the kitchen fire when part of the kitchen floor collapsed before her eyes, and a man's head popped up out of the floor telling her to not be afraid, as they were tunnelling under the house in the hope of alleviating the damp.[24]

While Williamson was particularly public about matters of principle, he very much kept his religious beliefs to himself. There are a few reasons however for us to accept that he may have had a personal faith in Christianity.

Firstly Stonehouse recalls a lady of his acquaintance who once approached Williamson while he was reading a book. He became shy when asked about the book, but eventually was pressed into revealing its title – it was a copy of the Bible.

The lady who was previously only familiar with the sharp-tongued Williamson of the public man, was shocked to witness a show of his sensitivity as he explained to her thoughtfully, 'The Bible tells me what a rascal I am.'[25]

On another occasion he confided with a local minister that he regretted having not gone into the priesthood in his youth, as he felt that he could have become a bishop. The minister however merely resorted to punning on his actual life's work by telling him, 'Oh! You would certainly have deserved to be an archbishop.'[26]

It may be significant that one of Williamson's first major tunnels in his subterranean labyrinth connected his home with the crypt of St. Mary's church, and was reputedly constructed to prevent himself and his wife from getting wet on rainy Sunday mornings.

---

[24] Stonehouse, J.; *The Streets of Liverpool* (1879), p136
[25] Williamson, J.; quote taken from Stonehouse, J.; *Recollections of Old Liverpool* (1863), p173.
[26] Whittington-Egan, R.; *Liverpool Characters and Eccentrics* (1985), p9.

This tunnel may well be a clue to the revelation of Williamson as a man of secretive prayer and contemplation – a sensitive man whose personality prevented him from openly expressing his religious beliefs, but whose personal connection to the church ended up being manifested in the most literal manner.

However it is probably more likely that the tunnel was simply a means of making a cultural necessity significantly more comfortable – especially when we consider this in connection with historian Charles R. Hand's description of the roads at Edge Hill around this time, 'In wet weather the lanes became stagnant pools and foot passengers carried armfuls of stones to fill them up.'[27]

It is also known that Williamson donated some of the excavated sandstone from the tunnel complex to build St. Jude's Church in 1831 on Montague Street – now the site of the Liverpool Royal Infirmary.

This could also be cited as an example of the manifestation of his religious beliefs, however it would not hold a strong argument. Firstly because he used the sandstone in the construction of a lot of buildings of his own on Mason Street – and certainly needed to find a use for what must have been a considerable amount of sandstone that he excavated from his subterranean follies.

Secondly because there was little chance of his being able to sell the stone as there was an abundance of available sandstone following the construction of Stephenson's railway tunnels in the 1830s, and technically the Crown owned the mineral rights to the land that he was excavating anyway.

We should by now be forming a strong sense of the type of man Williamson was, having examined his personality and beliefs. However it should be remembered that much of Williamson's persona as we understand it today is to some extent the construct of

---

[27] Hand, C. R.; *History of Edge Hill* (1920) - quote taken from *The Mole* magazine, Issue 2, p8.

numerous generations of historians, who have added to this portrait of 'eccentricity', each being influenced by their predecessor's versions of the tale.

When we consider that James Stonehouse was the first historian to write on the subject after Williamson's death, taking into account his dubious sources, we can begin to realise just how distorted our view of Williamson may actually be.

The reputed quotations that Stonehouse presents to us from Williamson and the 'Queen of Edge Hill' in particular, are concerning – and it would not seem too pessimistic to presume that much of these quotations are Stonehouse's own elaborations based vaguely on both his own and other people's memories of actual conversations. In such ways legends are made.

Even if we could be certain that these 'conversations' were accurate we must also remember that both Williamson and the 'Queen of Edge Hill' may be guilty of elaborating as a means of immortalising themselves into local folklore. Jean Peneff claims that:

> ...no life story should be taken a priori to be an authentic account. You have to adjust the screen of what is said and portrayed; you have to judge the degree of distortion, the strength of the refraction, just as physicists calculate the angle that a prism gives to a ray of light.[28]

The possibility of this sort of distortion can be seen particularly in descriptions of Williamson's actual appearance. The 'Queen of Edge Hill' presented a vivid description of him:

> ...his outward garments were threadbare and patched, and seemed to ill accord with the fine white shirt and extremely fine white flannel waistcoat that

---

[28] Peneff, J.; *op.cit.*, p41.

was perceptible. His mode of walking was remarkable; it was not exactly walking, but stumping, while his loud, roaring voice might have been heard a long way off...[29]

In his 1863 work James Stonehouse recalls that:

> Mr. Williamson's appearance was remarkable. His hat was what might have been truly called "a shocking bad one." He generally wore an old and very much patched brown coat, corduroy breeches, and thick, slovenly shoes; but his underclothing was always of the finest description, and faultless in cleanliness and colour. His manners were ordinarily rough and uncouth, speaking gruffly, bawling loudly, and even rudely when he did not take to any one.[30]

The two descriptions seem to match well, however perhaps surprisingly, Stonehouse goes on to claim that, 'His fine, well-shaped, muscular figure fully six feet high, his handsome head and face made him, when well-dressed, present a really distinguished appearance.'[31] Williamson well-dressed however, seems to have been a rare occasion. A writer in *The Rambler* of April 8, 1837 (notably published during Williamson's lifetime) recalls that Williamson:

> ... being jocosely remarked for his singular dress on 'chase, replied, 'What does it matter? Why, every one knows me here!' Some time subsequently, being in London, the very gentleman who before rallied him, met him on the Stock Exchange, in his usual habiliments, 'What, Joseph, have you made no

---

[29] Quoted by Stonehouse, J.; *The Excavations at Edge Hill.* (1858), p16.
[30] Stonehouse, J.; *Recollections of Old Liverpool* (1863), p171.
[31] *ibid.*

change in your wardrobe even in the city?' 'Pooh,' said our hero, dryly, 'Since no one knows me here!'[32]

Stonehouse was however accurate in believing that Williamson was capable of refinement when necessary. The most notable example of this was on the occasion of the Prince of Wales' (later George IV) visit to Liverpool in 1806. This is recorded clearly later in the article from *The Rambler*:

> ... when the Prince of Wales paid a visit to the 'Good Old Town' our citizens, unaccustomed to the presence of Royalty, and but young in the school of etiquette, hesitated in the mode of giving the Prince a welcome. The situation was awkward and the town was fast sinking in the Royal visitor's estimation, when Mr. Williamson stepped from the embarrassed crowd, and with that frank and native politeness that always distinguished him, bade his Prince welcome in the name of Liverpool, and thus rescued it from everlasting reproach. 'The most accomplished gentleman of the age' (as the Prince Regent was called) felt so pleased with his host's manner that he afterwards said that 'Mr. Williamson was the only gentleman in Liverpool'[33]

Williamson's tendency towards eccentric constructions manifested itself above the ground before the tunnel complex took hold of his imagination. The houses that he built on Mason Street and on a few of the surrounding roads seem to have been curious constructions in their own right. It is known that Williamson never made plans of the houses before they were built, but rather directed his men as they went along.

---

[32] *The Rambler*; 8th April 1837 - quote taken from Hand, Charles R.; *A History of Edge Hill* (1920), p50.
[33] *ibid*.

The result was that all of the houses were individual – a feature noted by Stonehouse, who wrote:

> Some of the backs of the Mason Street houses project, some recede, some have no windows visible, others have windows of such length and breadth as must have thrown any feeble-minded tax-gatherer when he had to receive window duty into fits. These houses really appear as if built by chance, or by a blind man who has felt his way and been satisfied with the security of his dwelling rather than its appearance.[34]

Williamson's unwillingness to produce plans of his houses for his builders did, as one might expect, lead to mistakes being made. The most bizarre example of this occurred when Williamson and his men forgot to include a fireplace, a window and even a door in one room.[35]

Realising his mistake Williamson made a shaft through an upper room with a skylight above in order to give the room some light. The introduction of a fireplace proved too burdensome a task for Williamson, who eventually decided to leave it out altogether. Quite how it was possible to overlook the inclusion of a door into the room is frankly beyond my comprehension. However we are assured by Stonehouse that, '…the utmost ingenuity was obliged to be exercised to introduce it at all.'[36]

One of Williamson's most famous tenants was the portrait painter Cornelius Henderson, who was also a great friend of Williamson.

Once, while in conversation with Williamson, Henderson had complained of the bad light that he had to paint in. In typical style

---

[34] Stonehouse, J.; *Recollections of Old Liverpool* (1863), p192.
[35] Stonehouse, J.; *The Streets of Liverpool* (1879), p144.
[36] *ibid.*

Williamson assured him that he could solve his friend's problem within a short time.

Thinking little of the conversation Henderson went about his business for the next few weeks quite unaware of the surprise his friend was preparing for him. Eventually it was completed and so Williamson took his friend to the corner of Bolton Street (now Shimmin Street). Here Henderson was most shocked to discover that Williamson had built an enormous house complete with immense windows, for him to use as a studio.

Obviously touched by this incredible and undoubtedly extremely expensive display of friendship Henderson must have found it difficult to explain to Williamson that it was not the quantity of light which was important to an artist, but rather the quality of it.

Upon hearing this Williamson is said to have fallen into an immense rage with Henderson, swearing at him, and finding it impossible to understand the differentiation between quantity and quality of light.

The Reverend Hull, who was passing and heard the commotion attempted to calm Williamson's temper, and explained that Henderson was indeed correct in his unfortunate revelation.

However Williamson merely complained, '…here's light, plenty for everything and anything, and yet he says it's of no use to him.'[37]

Henderson never moved into the house, but luckily it seems that their friendship was no more diminished for the misunderstanding. The house however stood for many years uninhabited, as Williamson in his excitement had omitted to include either a kitchen or any other homely conveniences.

Williamson's haphazard constructions on Edge Hill however, merely reflect his preoccupation with the ingenuity of the

---

[37] *ibid.*, p136.

constructions taking place beneath Edge Hill. There can be little doubt that for the final two decades of his life Williamson's greatest passion was for his subterranean labyrinth – and the greatest craftsmanship of his men was being displayed in the caverns and vaults deep below the ground where few people would ever see them.

Williamson very rarely allowed anybody to explore the tunnel system, claiming as he did that, 'These are not show stops and I am not a showman'.[38]

However in 1839 he did grant permission to Dr. George C. Watson to explore the labyrinth. Dr. Watson was a well-known physician who regularly wrote letters on sanitary reform in the *Liverpool Standard* under the pseudonym of 'Medicus'.

Upon being granted permission to explore the tunnels Williamson gave him a note to prove that he had been permitted into the tunnels, so rare was the honour. The note read:

> Dr. Watson is not to be interrupted in his walks on my premises, either on the surface or under the surface.
> 7th August 1839
> J.W., E.H.[39]

Dr. Watson is believed to have been quite shocked by the great extent of the tunnel system and by the quality of craftsmanship that was displayed in its construction. The excellence of Williamson's tradesmen was also noticed by another famous contemporary of Williamson – George Stephenson.

Throughout the 1830s the eminent engineer George Stephenson was occupied in the construction of the Liverpool and Manchester

---

[38] Williamson, J.; quoted by Whale, D.; *Lost Villages of Liverpool - Part Two* (1984), p42.
[39] Quoted by Stonehouse, J.; *The Excavations at Edge Hill.* (1858), p22.

railway – one of the earliest public railway lines in the world, and the test site for the award-winning locomotive the 'Rocket'.

In 1834 as part of the line's extension through to the new Lime Street station Stephenson's men were occupied in the construction of a major tunnel through Edge Hill – quite unaware of the area's already vibrant subterranean activities.

The tunnel in fact, which was later opened into a cutting, passed directly beneath Williamson's land. Williamson was almost certainly aware of this, and probably quite deliberately had his men dig a tunnel under Stephenson's new construction.

As Stephenson's men worked away deep under the ground the floor of their tunnel began to collapse before their eyes, and the robust figure of Williamson is reputed to have stepped up to greet them.

It has been reasonably suggested by a few historians that many of the workers must have believed, if only for a moment, that they'd unwittingly burrowed into the first circles of Hell, to be greeted by the Devil himself.

Their baffled expressions must have been quite an amusement to Williamson, who brushing himself down, told them that, '…if they wanted to know how to tunnel he could give them a lesson in that polite art.'[40]

After this typically comical introduction it is known that Williamson and Stephenson became good friends – each filled with admiration for the other's works.

Williamson allowed Stephenson the unusual honour of a complete tour around his tunnel system, and Stephenson is believed to have been most impressed by the workmanship of the

---

[40] Stonehouse, J.; *The Streets of Liverpool* (1879), p139.

construction, saying (much to Williamson's delight) that they were, '...the most astonishing works he had ever seen in their way.'[41]

It is a wonderfully poetic irony, when we remember Williamson's original reasons for building the labyrinth, that Stephenson then went on to employ many of Williamson's men in the construction of his railway tunnels.

Many men remained indebted to Williamson for work however until May 1, 1840, when the great 'King of Edge Hill' died at the age of seventy-one from 'water on the chest'.[42]

Williamson was buried with his wife Elizabeth in the Tate family vault at St. Thomas's Church, which stood at the junction of Paradise Street and Park Lane, and was where the couple married some thirty-eight years earlier.

The church was eventually demolished in 1906 and all of the graves except the Tate family vault were exhumed and removed. Either because of the size of the vault or because there were no remaining family members alive to cover the cost of the exhumation the Tate family vault was left at the junction.

For many years Liverpool's greatest philanthropist lay with his wife and her family almost completely forgotten at an unmarked point beneath a waste-ground car park.

But in 2006 regeneration work in the area saw the ground dug over for the construction of a new retail development. During the work Williamson's tomb stone was discovered. It was photographed and reburied. At the time of writing plans are afoot to build a permanent marker for the great man's final resting place.

---

[41] Stephenson, G.; Quoted by Moran, S.; *The Dawn of the Railway Age* (1997) - published in *The Mole* magazine, Issue 2, p5.
[42] Whale, D.; *Lost Villages of Liverpool - Part 2* (1984), p43.

At the time of his death Williamson's fortune is said to have stood at £40,000, and it has been estimated that he had probably spent somewhere in the region of £100,000 in paying his worker's wages.[43]

It is believed that in the last eighteen years of his life – following his wife's death, Williamson took to living in the area of the tunnel system beneath his home.

A fireplace still exists in this area and whilst this lifestyle may have been reclusive it was probably fairly comfortable.

James Stonehouse however, in one of his more sensationalist moments described these subterranean living quarters as, '...more like the den for a wild beast than the dwelling place of a human being.'[44]

A more accurate way of judging his lifestyle is to study the catalogue of the auction of his belongings that took place on June 7, 1841.

This shows him as a cultured and comfortable man living in a richly furnished home. Even just a short excerpt from the list can clarify this, '...the remaining part of the household furniture, two capital eight-day clocks, Semi-Grand Pianoforte by Stodart, pedal harp, a valuable collection of paintings and engravings, library of books...'[45]

We also know that Williamson had been cared for by his faithful housekeeper, who had actually married Williamson's friend Cornelius Henderson.

---

[43] Whittington-Egan, R.; *Liverpool Characters and Eccentrics* (1985), p12.
[44] Stonehouse, J.; *The Excavations at Edge Hill.* (1858), p14.
[45] Hand, C. R.; *History of Edge Hill* (1920), p51.

We can presume that Mrs. Henderson had been a reliable housekeeper as Williamson left her a generous annuity in his will of £300.[46]

A week after his death the *Liverpool Mercury* printed a lengthy obituary to Williamson that appears to mock him quite disrespectfully considering his recent demise.

It stands as a shocking example of how his philanthropy was misunderstood, and refers to him as the 'mole' rather than the 'king' of Edge Hill – a cruelly sarcastic demotion, and a title which has invariably stuck:

> ...Mr. Williamson was a person of eccentric habits, and well known in his neighbourhood by a peculiar and to all persons but himself seemingly ridiculous propensity of making expensive excavations under the earth. In the pursuit of this propensity he has spent large sums of money. He seemed anxious to realise what the late Mr. Cobbett used to quiz the House of Lords for having once recommended, by way of finding employment for the poor – digging holes one day and filling them in the next. Mr. Williamson in the pursuit of this strange habit, has vaulted and undermined the greatest portion of Mason Street, Edge Hill ... amidst all his eccentricities and mole like propensities, he had some good points in his character, although there was no reckoning with any certainty upon what he would do under any given circumstances ... we should not have been surprised had he left orders that his body should be buried in one of his catacombs, for which no earthly use has ever been assigned.[47]

---

[46] Hand, C.R.; 'Joseph Williamson: The King of Edge Hill' (1916), in *Transactions of the Historic Society of Lancashire and Cheshire* (1917) Volume 68, R. & R. Clark Ltd. (Edinburgh), p2.
[47] *Liverpool Mercury*; 8th May 1840.

In the years following Williamson's death the grandeur of Edge Hill steadily declined and poverty in the area developed rapidly as the wealthy residents moved away.

Stonehouse claims that this deterioration commenced with, 'The erection of a set of court houses over an old deft, skirted by Upper Mason Street, about 1845,'[48]

These small terraced houses, packed into courtyards were notoriously horrendous habitations, and were viewed by many as a threat to public health.

Sanitation was a growing issue at this time in the city championed by people such as Dr. Watson (who had been allowed through the tunnels in Williamson's lifetime) and most famously Dr. Duncan, who became Liverpool's first Public Health Officer.

The area of course at this time had no organised system for the removal of rubbish and soon Williamson's disused tunnel system became the popular dumping place for all of the residents' waste.

An even greater concern was that the area had no sewerage system at this time and so human effluence was generally also dumped into the tunnel system.

This problem was reported in the Liverpool journal *The Porcupine* in 1867, and the Medical Officer of Health had apparently, '...highlighted the unpleasant risk of disease which existed at the back of Mason Street.'[49]

This was noted by James Stonehouse, who in 1879 illustrated how the tunnel system had not only become a threat to public health, but also a serious threat to public safety:

---

[48] Stonehouse, J.; *The Streets of Liverpool* (1879), p130.
[49] *The Mole* magazine, Issue 6, p7.

> The effluvium hereabouts at one time was very obnoxious. There was a run of water from the lowest of one of the arches. In one place a deep well was excavated, into which a woman one night fell and was drowned.[50]

Throughout this time Williamson's unusual buildings on Mason Street were slowly being demolished as they became less practical to the area's needs. Often the unwanted buildings were knocked down and the rubble would be discarded into the tunnel system.

In the century following Williamson's death therefore the tunnels became increasingly inaccessible. Ironically this inaccessibility has probably been a great aid in the preservation of the tunnel system, and should the multitudinous layers of rubble be painstakingly removed today the original tunnels are probably in a good condition.

The unfortunate result though is that for the moment a great deal of the labyrinth is inaccessible, but luckily a number of explorers since Williamson's death have recorded their ventures into the tunnel system.

The earliest of these is James Stonehouse who explored the tunnels within the first decades following Williamson's death, and so is able to provide us with the most comprehensive survey. Yet even he is unable to furnish us with a complete vision of the tunnel system in its prime, as he wrote in 1863:

> It must be a matter of great regret that after Mr. Williamson's death, someone able to make an accurate survey of the property did not go through and describe it, because it has been greatly changed since then by the accumulations of rubbish that have been brought to every part of it.[51]

---

[50] Stonehouse, J.; *The Streets of Liverpool* (1879), p143.
[51] Stonehouse, J.; *Recollections of Old Liverpool* (1863), p187.

The tunnel system has however been dramatically altered since Stonehouse wrote this. He recorded an immensely detailed account of the labyrinth at the time of his explorations, and also produced a map to accompany his writings.

The basic fact to be learnt from Stonehouse's writings seems to be that there were four sorts of subterranean construction in the system.

Firstly there were the vaulted archways that supported the gardens at the back of the Mason Street houses. From these, large tunnels developed back into the sandstone beneath the buildings. Secondly there were the cellars to the houses that Williamson constructed. He often built incredibly deep foundations for his buildings, which were then constructed into layers of cellars. Many of his buildings were as deep below the ground as they were high above it (up to six stories in each direction).

Thirdly there were obscure caverns, immense in size, deep below the ground – the most famous being known as Williamson's 'Banqueting Hall'. These three types of construction were then linked by a complex series of tunnels which varied greatly in size and construction – ranging from large tunnels vaulted with intricate brickwork arches, to passages cut into the rock only just large enough for a person to squeeze through.

Stonehouse tells us of a large tunnel opening onto Smithdown Lane that would have been used by Williamson's men as the main route for the extraction of the excavated sandstone. He writes:

> ...there was a strong archway, with solid folding doors ... this was the entrance to a tunnel, or vaulted passage, through which the carts brought up the stone from the great quarry. It would admit of two wagons abreast. It was higher at the eastern than at the western end. On the outer surface was soil with

bushes growing. This vast arch or passage is now destroyed.[52]

In an earlier piece he describes the tunnel as:

> ...in shape like a seaman's speaking trumpet ... it gradually deepens at the eastern end, and is about 15 feet wide, and 26 high. At the opening it is not more than 15 high.[53]

Apart from just providing us with historical information on long lost features of the labyrinth, Stonehouse's writing is also capable of communicating the atmosphere of the place:

> ...a strange place it is ... vaulted passages cut out of the solid rock; arches thrown up by craftsman's hands, beautiful in proportion and elegant in form, but supporting nothing. Tunnels formed here – deep pits there. Yawning gulfs where the fetid, stagnant waters threw up their baneful odours ... and there, vaulted over, is a gulf that makes the brain dizzy, and strikes us with terror as we look down into it.[54]

Stonehouse, perhaps typically as a Victorian historian, greatly romanticises the place in his use of florid language and awe-struck descriptions. His glorification of arches as 'beautiful in proportion and elegant in form'[55] reflect the contemporary appeal in industrialised Victorian Britain for the splendour of craftsmanship, and the victory of human construction over nature. His dramatic metaphors such as 'yawning gulfs'[56] empower the sense of mystery and add the subtle suggestion of a supernatural factor to the tunnel system.

---

[52] Stonehouse, J.; *The Streets of Liverpool* (1879), p140.
[53] Stonehouse, J.; *Recollections of Old Liverpool* (1863), p189.
[54] *ibid.*, p186.
[55] *ibid.*
[56] *ibid.*

At the beginning of the 20th century local historian Charles R. Hand wrote a number of pieces on the tunnels and is also known to have explored the labyrinth. On the 3rd February 1916 Hand read a lecture on the subject to the Historic Society of Lancashire and Cheshire.[57] The main part of this was the reading of a piece by Stonehouse that had been written for the Society more than half a century before.

However Stonehouse had not delivered the lecture, having received threats from Cornelius Henderson to take proceedings against the historian for trespass and libel on Williamson's character, should the speech be read. This alone suggests a possible degree of inaccuracy in Stonehouse's writings on Williamson.

An article in the *Daily Post* on November 15, 1925, reports of how the Liverpool Historic Society, led by Charles R. Hand explored the tunnels beneath 126 Paddington, Edge Hill. The party was reported to have explored for nearly a mile before returning back to their original entrance. Incredibly there are a number of photographs from this expedition which reveal areas of the labyrinth that are not accessible today.

In 1902 the headquarters of the First Lancashire Royal Engineers were built on part of Williamson's land. It is believed that the Royal Engineers used some of the larger underground caverns as a site for practising their skills in the construction of bridges.[58]

In 1907 with the land still owned by the army the West Lancashire Territorial Forces Association produced a map of the tunnel system. The project was probably part of their training, but has left us with a clear map of the system at this time that illustrates how many of the passages had become inaccessible since

---

[57] Hand, C.R.; 'Joseph Williamson: The King of Edge Hill' (1916), in *Transactions of the Historic Society of Lancashire and Cheshire* (1917) Volume 68, R. & R. Clark Ltd. (Edinburgh).
[58] According to *The Mole* magazine, Issue 3, p11.

Stonehouse's map had been produced. They also produced a cross-section diagram that illustrates the varying depths of the tunnels.

During the Second World War the local authorities inspected the tunnels to see if they were suitable for air raid shelters or munitions stores, however probably because of the amount of rubble in them they were deemed inappropriate for either.

By the late 1960s another local historian, Richard Whittington-Egan had explored the tunnels. He later wrote that:

> ...scattered about in perilous plenitude were hungry pits and yawning chasms that seemed to cry silently for the vengeful engulfing of any who would ignore their presence ... for the trespasser, the dangers were myriad.[59]

It is interesting to note that by this period what had begun as an occasional metaphor in Stonehouse's descriptions is in Whittington-Egan a labyrinth itself of linguistic devices.

The anthropomorphic description of the chasms as 'yawning'[60] reflects Stonehouse's earlier use of the same metaphor, but the suggestion of a supernatural element to the labyrinth has become explicit with Whittington-Egan's assertion that the chasms 'seemed to cry silently for the vengeful engulfing of any who would ignore their presence'.[61]

We have to ask ourselves what has happened here to the historicisation of the labyrinth within the century between Stonehouse and Whittington-Egan.

---

[59] Whittington-Egan, R.; *Liverpool Characters and Eccentrics* (1985), p8.
[60] *ibid.*
[61] *ibid.*

The narrative has developed from being an attempt to historicise the site, to being a purely entertaining mystery tale reflecting the period's compulsion towards the supernatural and the mysterious.

Subsequently we are presented with this narrative in which dramatic construction appears to be more significant than historical accuracy.

In his celebrated work *Mythologies*, Roland Barthes claims that, 'Myth deprives the object of which it speaks of all history. In it, history evaporates.'[62]

In the development of the Williamson myth we can clearly see a movement away from a clinical documentation of events towards a more dramatic narrative. However we should not lose sight of the fact that the development of the local folklore around the Williamson myth is as much an integral part of the history of the tunnel system as the raw facts about its physical construction.

Most locals have heard of the tunnels at some point, but with an absence of any recent definitive histories of Williamson and his labyrinth, few people know little more than what seems to be the vaguest of legends.

As with all legends however local society has picked-up on the mysterious tales of the 'Mole of Edge Hill'. For example a pub was opened recently in the area bearing this title. Similarly a children's novel was published in 1955 which was set in and around the tunnel system.

The book is no longer in print, and is now very difficult to get hold of, but does act as a fascinating example of how the local culture uses the legend.

---

[62] Barthes, R.; *Mythologies* (1957), Vintage Books (London) – trans. by A. Lavers (1993), p151.

Written by Kathleen Fidler, the story of *The Deans Defy Danger* is similar in style to Enid Blyton's 'Famous Five' series. After discovering an ancient treasure map the children at the centre of the tale find themselves in a subterranean, swash-buckling adventure through the labyrinth, which follows all of the usual constraints of the genre. The majority of the representation of the tunnel system itself however is surprisingly accurate – Fidler almost certainly using the works of Stonehouse and Hand as reference. At one stage the famous 'Banqueting Hall' is certainly recognisable:

> They were in what seemed to be a great hall, with the walls hewn out of the solid rock, but the roof was of bricked arches. At the far end was a heap of stones and rubble, which did not quite hide another passage leading from the cavern.[63]

In more recent years a number of geophysics surveys have been carried out in the area in an attempt to ascertain the present state of the tunnel complex.

Since 1995 teams from Bangor University, Lancaster University and Liverpool University have all attempted to map the labyrinth using micro-gravity surveying equipment. These projects have generally correlated fairly well with earlier maps, however what seems to be a number of previously unknown tunnels have also been discovered.

By the mid 1990s, the tunnels had become a charged issue in Liverpool with a great debate being voiced over their future.

In 1996 a large portion of the land above the tunnel system, previously derelict, was bought by a property development company who intended to use the land for the construction of student flats. By the beginning of 1997 the Friends of Williamson's Tunnels Society had set themselves up in opposition to this development, fearing that

---

[63] Fidler, K.; *The Deans Defy Danger* (1955) – extract taken from *The Mole* magazine, Issue 4, p4.

it would involve the destruction of many of the tunnels as well as the Lord Mayor's Stable Yard on Smithdown Lane – an historic site in its own right. But this group, made up of local enthusiasts, proposed that the tunnel system could be better redeveloped as a tourist attraction.

In the first issue of the Friends Of Williamson's Tunnels quarterly magazine *The Mole*, editor Bill Douglas wrote:

> Remember, the Albert Dock was only saved from the bulldozers by the frantic last minute campaigning of enthusiasts and that is now one of the top tourist attractions in Britain.[64]

The situation was made more confusing by the fact that the property development company – Seymour Properties of Winsford, who owned the site (covering approximately a third of the tunnel complex) set up their own fundraising wing – The Joseph Williamson Society.

This society was designed to gain funding (from organisations such as English Partnerships) in order to renovate a small part of the tunnel system as a tourist attraction. Under this plan an area of the tunnel system, leading from the Double Tunnel entrance could be opened to the public.

The official response from the Friends of Williamson's Tunnels seemed to suggest peace was at last descending on Edge Hill once again:

> Whilst welcoming the idea of renovating and opening the corner tunnel and double tunnel, we believe that all the tunnels under this part of the site should be excavated, renovated and opened to the public. If the method of doing this is to open some tunnels first and the rest later, that, in theory, is fine so long as (I)

---

[64] Douglas, Bill; *The Mole* magazine, Issue 1, p2.

there are guarantees that the unexcavated tunnels will be unharmed by the construction work and (II) the unexcavated tunnels are accessible for future excavations.[65]

With the arrival of the new decade and the new millennium, this project finally got under way. The Williamson's Tunnels tourist attraction now has an impressive glass frontage covering the face of the double tunnels. With a café, and information centre, and regular guided walks, the public can now enjoy Williamson's great creations.

Other areas of the tunnel system also underwent changes before the turn of the 21st century.

The Paddington Gardens area, which is believed to include some of the most intricate parts of Williamson's labyrinth, became a hive of activity as a separate student housing development began to take shape.

The developers designed their construction to be tunnel-friendly – the new flats were built over the foundations of the previous 1930s tenement blocks, and so did not disturb the tunnel system.

However in February 1999 these contractors unexpectedly uncovered cellars and caverns that were part of the labyrinth. In the *Liverpool Echo* of February 10, 1999 Steve Moran, Joint Secretary of the Friends of Williamson's Tunnels explained, 'There are two cellars, one above the other and next to that is another large 'L' shaped cavern which was filled-in in 1937 when the original flats were built.'[66] The developers promised to protect the cellars by rafting over them before laying the foundations for the new flats.

During this period, the area of the tunnel system around Mason Street also saw redevelopment as the Friends of Williamson's

---

[65] Douglas, Bill; *The Mole* magazine, Issue 7, p2.
[66] Moran, Steve; *Liverpool Echo* – 10th February 1999.

Tunnels took on the remains of Williamson's house (only the front façade of the original building remains) with the intention of occasionally opening this central part of the tunnel system to the public.

There is a poetic irony to the redevelopment of the labyrinth as a tourist attraction – as the process brings an enormous amount of both temporary and permanent employment to the area – so that Williamson's original reasons for creating the tunnels in an earlier time of economic uncertainty could be ingeniously recycled.

Williamson's life and works seem fascinating as a portrait of success, eccentricity and philanthropy, but equally fascinating is the manner in which this character has been treated by generations of historians since his death – the Victorian pre-occupation with glorified notions of the self-made man – the entrepreneur turned philanthropist; the early twentieth century rationalist historians who obsess on the question of why Williamson chose to build a labyrinth of all things; the mid-twentieth century postmodernist historians who attempt to encapsulate the experience of the tunnels in a new labyrinth of drawn-out metaphors and similes.

Today we have the local history societies, desperate to map, document and even restore the labyrinth – as its value is as an integral part of their local identity.

Finally, of course I have added to this cumulative history in my own analysis which I hope constitutes some sense of all of these previous historicisations with the additional concentration upon the historicisation of the myth surrounding Williamson's tunnels, and its relationship to both the society responsible for its creation, and the actual known history of the site.

Luisa Passerini in her work *Mythbiography in Oral History* notes that:

> We are in the position, since we live in an epoch of de-industrialisation, of historicising the myth and its

impact: finding its origins, studying its trajectory, analysing the signs of its end.[67]

Charles R. Hand concludes his chapter on Williamson in his unpublished *History of Edge Hill* (1920), by telling us that:

> A stroll along Mason Street at the present time is a rather depressing experience. The courts on the east side are uninhabited and boarded up, but here and there are still to be seen old buildings of strange and uncouth appearance, suggestive of the genius of the man who excavated caves, vaults, tunnels and passages that led to nothing. Beyond the signalling station of the Engineers, and looking westward, the land presents a desolate appearance, and on the lower extremity it can be identified by the huge unused ventilating shaft of the railway which runs beneath, and which intersected Williamson's tunnels. Not far from this ungainly structure, Garden Street, off Smithdown Lane, commemorates in a way Mr. Mason's beautiful gardens, which before Williamson's time occupied the hill side, but there are no flowers there now.[68]

People don't stroll along Mason Street today, but if you do it is fair to say that it is still a depressing experience. The courts (terraced houses set out in a series of courtyards) to which Hand refers are long gone, and apart from a section of the front façade of Williamson's house, there are no buildings left to remind us of this singular character – the 'buildings of strange and uncouth appearance' which Hand saw in 1920 have been reduced to rubble one by one.

---

[67] Passerini, L.; 'Mythbiography in Oral History' (1990) in *The Myths We Live By* (1990), Routledge (London), p52.
[68] Hand, C. R.; *History of Edge Hill* (1920), p53.

The Royal Engineers have, at some earlier moment in the sepia past, demobilised and left the area leaving no apparent trace of their ever having been there.

The huge ventilating shaft of the railway, unused even as Hand strolled, is now nowhere to be seen. The 1930s tenement blocks, undreamt of in 1920, have even been demolished before our eyes in a frenzy of noise and dust.

A stroll along Mason Street today is a sort of apocalyptic experience – making it difficult to imagine the street in all of its nineteenth century glory and grandeur. However deep below the ground, our footsteps are echoing through a great maze of tunnels, vaults, caverns and chambers.

This labyrinth kingdom of Edge Hill's most colourful resident lies quietly waiting to be rediscovered.

Explored by a new age of locals – equally in need of employment as their forefathers, and maybe one-day equally as indebted to Joseph Williamson for providing it.

Also by the author:

Island Life: A History of Looe Island

Looe Island enchants all who visit, with its beauty and tranquillity. But the island's history is full of mystery and intrigue.

In Island Life: A History of Looe Island, writer David Clensy reveals the island's many unknown secrets - from its early monastic inhabitants, to the sinister 18th century smugglers who used it as a place to land and stow their booty.

Discover how the island witnessed the opening shots against the Spanish Armada, and was bombed during the Second World War.

The author brings us up to date, with an affectionate portrait of the indomitable Atkins sisters, who lived on the island for more than 30 years.

Available now from www.amazon.co.uk and all good book shops

or direct from the publishers at www.lulu.com

For more information:

www.looeisland.com